✶ SUPERLOO ✶

HADRIAN'S
Lucky Latrine

Toilets run in W. C. Flushing's family. His gran, the formidable Dame Netty Flushing, was a tireless campaigner for a public convenience in every town. It was she who inspired his lifelong love of lavatories. 'Thanks to Dame Netty,' W. C. Flushing recalls fondly, 'my entire life has been toilets.'

W. C. Flushing is best known for his great ten-volume work, *Our Toilet Heritage.*

Dedicated to my gran,
Dame Netty Flushing,
whom I shall alw

'A breath of fresh
– *My Lav*

D1059496

HADRIAN'S
Lucky Latrine

W. C. Flushing

Illustrated by Martin Chatterton

PUFFIN

PUFFIN BOOKS

Published by the Penguin Group
Penguin Books Ltd, 80 Strand, London WC2R 0RL, England
Penguin Group (USA) Inc., 375 Hudson Street, New York, New York 10014, USA
Penguin Group (Canada), 90 Eglinton Avenue East, Suite 700, Toronto, Ontario,
Canada M4P 2Y3 (a division of Pearson Penguin Canada Inc.)
Penguin Ireland, 25 St Stephen's Green, Dublin 2, Ireland
(a division of Penguin Books Ltd)
Penguin Group (Australia), 250 Camberwell Road, Camberwell, Victoria 3124,
Australia (a division of Pearson Australia Group Pty Ltd)
Penguin Books India Pvt Ltd, 11 Community Centre, Panchsheel Park,
New Delhi – 110 017, India
Penguin Group (NZ), cnr Airborne and Rosedale Roads, Albany, Auckland 1310,
New Zealand (a division of Pearson New Zealand Ltd)
Penguin Books (South Africa) (Pty) Ltd, 24 Sturdee Avenue, Rosebank,
Johannesburg 2196, South Africa

Penguin Books Ltd, Registered Offices: 80 Strand, London WC2R 0RL, England

www.penguin.com

First published 2006
2

Text copyright © Susan Gates, 2006
Illustrations copyright © Martin Chatterton, 2006
All rights reserved

The moral right of the author and illustrator has been asserted

Set in Baskerville MT by Palimpsest Book Production Limited
Polmont, Stirlingshire
Made and printed in England by Clays Ltd, St Ives plc

British Library Cataloguing in Publication Data
A CIP catalogue record for this book is available from the British Library

ISBN-13: 978-0-141-32005-2
ISBN-10: 0-141-32005-2

CHAPTER ONE

'No way,' said Finn. 'I'm not coming with you. Never again. Those missions to rescue your relatives are far too scary.'

His voice echoed round the tiny metal cubicle: *Scary – scary – scary!*

Finn was inside a toilet. One of those super-loos you find in town centres, that look like shiny space-age pods and clean themselves between customers. And can even say, when you've finished, 'Don't forget to flush.'

But the loo Finn was in was much smarter than that. It made those other loos look like dummies. By mistake, in the superloo factory it had been fitted with the wrong microchip. Now it could time-travel. It had a brain as big as a planet. And it practically never stopped talking.

Its quacky robot voice was booming out now from the speakers in its ceiling.

'I'm off to Roman Britain,' Superloo told Finn. 'To the North of England where the Emperor Hadrian built his great Wall. This trip will be a breeze,' it bragged. 'My giant computer brain has it all planned out to the last detail. There's practically no risk.'

'Oh yeah?' frowned Finn. 'Didn't you say that the last time? When I was nearly killed by a crazy Ancient Egyptian priest?'

Superloo pooh-poohed that idea. '*Cha!*' it said scornfully. 'You were never *really* in danger. Anyway, this time we won't hang around. We'll just whizz there. Grab the two toilets. Then whizz back. Easy-peasy!'

'*Two* toilets?' said Finn. He could have bitten off his tongue – he hadn't meant to show any interest.

'Yes!' crowed Superloo. 'Isn't it fabulous? I can save *two* ancient toilet relatives at the same time!'

It flashed its cubicle lights on and off and flushed its toilet bowl a few times to show how excited it was.

'Although, to be strictly accurate,' it added, 'they're not complete toilets. They're latrine seats, as used in forts by Roman soldiers.'

'I know about that!' said Finn. 'Roman

soldiers sat on latrines in long rows and they wiped their bums with . . .'

'Yes, yes, yes,' said Superloo impatiently. 'Every schoolchild remembers that. But here's the *really* important bit. One of these seats is from the actual latrine the Emperor Hadrian used on his first trip to Britain. But it's even more thrilling than that. It's the latrine he was sitting on when had his Big Idea.'

'What Big Idea?' Finn just couldn't help asking.

'The idea of building Hadrian's Wall, of course. The story goes, he was staying at the fort at Vindolanda, back in AD 123. Now Hadrian didn't stand on ceremony. He liked to share a laugh and a joke with the common soldiers. So there he was, in the latrines, chatting away, when suddenly he looked up – those latrines were open-air of course, it was less whiffy that way. Anyway, he gazed out over the wild rolling hills of what is now Northumberland. And he said, "This place needs a Wall!" He even carved some graffiti on the seat with his very own dagger: "It was on this Bog that Hadrian had his Big Idea."'

'*Humm*,' said Finn dubiously. 'Strange place to have great thoughts, if you ask me.'

'On the contrary,' cried Superloo. 'Some people find toilets very inspirational places. Don't you ever have Big Ideas on the toilet?'

'No!' snapped Finn.

He didn't want to encourage this discussion. What he did in the toilet was his business.

'And what about the other toilet – I mean, latrine seat?' asked Finn, anxious to change the subject. 'The other one you want to rescue?'

'Well, that's an exact replica of the wooden seat Hadrian sat on. Only it's made of gold and . . .'

'*Whoa, whoa,*' Finn chipped in. 'You're losing me here. Why did they make a golden copy?'

'To present to Hadrian, of course, when he came back, five years later, to inspect the finished Wall. You couldn't present an Emperor with a scruffy old wooden latrine seat, could you? And anyway, by then the *original* latrine seat was being used for something else.'

'Something else?' said Finn, looking puzzled. 'Like what else can you use a loo seat for?'

'Look, I'll explain properly when we get there,' said Superloo. 'We haven't got time now.'

'What's all this "we"?' asked Finn. 'I told you, I'm not coming! So don't try to make me.'

Immediately, the toilet began to snivel. 'But I need you!' it whined. 'You don't know what it's like being me, a genius trapped inside this ridiculous toilet body. I need your help.'

It gave a small choking sob.

'Don't you start crying!' Finn warned it. 'Don't you dare!'

He knew the wily toilet would use any means to persuade him: threats, flattery, tears. But this time he was wise to its tricks.

'For the last time, I'm not coming!' said Finn. 'And that's final.'

There was no answer from the super-intelligent loo.

'You're not sulking, are you?' Finn asked it.

It usually did when it couldn't get its own way.

'I'm going home then,' said Finn, 'if you're in a huff.'

He stepped out of the cubicle into the sunshine of the disused industrial estate. This was where Superloo lived. It had been left behind after the factories closed, forgotten by Hi-Tech Toilets, the firm that had made it.

Finn was stomping off through the weeds and rubble, thinking, *I should never have come.* That toilet was nothing but trouble. Suddenly he heard a *whooshing* sound behind him. And a muffled, quacky voice shrieking, 'Blast off! Britannica, here I come!'

Oh no! thought Finn, spinning around.

Where Superloo had been, there was just empty air.

'It's gone without me!' gasped Finn, dismayed. He'd refused to go with it. He hadn't given in to its wiles. So why did he feel so upset?

'I'm so excited!' warbled the toilet, as it whirled back through space and time.

It had gone into a sulk at first when Finn refused to come. But its massive self-confidence had soon come bouncing back.

'Humans only mess things up,' Superloo told itself, as it travelled. 'You're much better off on your own.'

Nevertheless, it did need humans, to carry out the rest of its plan. Two of them, preferably. No need to bring them all the way from the twenty-first century. It could pick them up here in Roman Britain.

'Perfect landing,' the loo congratulated itself, as with a soft thud it touched down.

It slid open its door with a *shush*, sneakily, as if it was setting a trap. Now all it had to do was wait.

CHAPTER TWO

For a while, nothing happened. Superloo's steel toilet bowl glittered. Paper in its jumbo bog-roll holder fluttered in the breeze.

Then a thought fizzed through its circuits: *There are humans coming!*

Superloo couldn't see. But it had super-sharp sensors in its floor and ceiling. They detected the tiniest sound and movement. It had a brilliant computer brain to analyse data. It didn't need eyes to know what was going on.

'The Roman army!' concluded Superloo smugly, as it sensed the ground being shaken by the *tramp, tramp, tramp* of a hundred metal-studded sandals. 'And, by my calculations, it should be the first cohort of the Fourth Legion, just coming back to their fort from patrol.'

Then came the clashing of weapons, an

order being shouted. It was in Latin. But that didn't bother Superloo. Its giant brain understood all languages.

A marching column of soldiers came out of the mist. It passed by without seeing Superloo, hidden by a grove of trees.

Two stragglers, limping along behind the column, plonked themselves down. They started talking. The time-travelling toilet listened in.

One took off his sandals, peeled off his thick hairy socks. 'My blisters are killing me!' He raked around in his kitbag. 'Don't say I forgot my ointment stick.'

'Look for it later,' said the other soldier. 'When we're back behind the Wall.'

He glanced nervously around. No Roman soldier liked being beyond the Wall. Hadrian's Wall cut right across Northern Britannica. To the South was civilization with the Romans, more or less, in charge. On the other side was unconquered wilderness, with bears, wolves and blue-painted savages who liked nailing their enemies' heads to their front doors.

The legionary shivered. 'Come on,' he urged his mate. 'It's not far to the fort. Look, you can see it from here.'

9

Their fort was one of sixteen that had been built along Hadrian's Wall. Already their cohort was clanking through its North Gate, trumpets blaring to tell everyone, 'We're back!' Their standard was raised proudly aloft. It looked remarkably like a wooden latrine seat.

The soldiers were talking again. From the grove of trees, Superloo listened in.

'I'm on whitewashing detail again,' said one. 'Clavus'll blow his top if I'm late.' Clavus was the most senior centurion at the fort – a battle-scarred veteran of many campaigns. You didn't mess with him if you knew what was good for you.

'Is there *anything* that's not being white-washed?' grumbled the other. 'The Wall, the bath house, even the barracks! Just so it all looks smart for the presentation.'

'It'll never be ready on time – that new amphitheatre is a real botched job. And the Emperor's arriving the day after tomorrow. That's when he gets presented with the latrine – the golden replica, that is.'

The cohort would never part with the real seat. After Hadrian's last visit, the latrine seat had been treated like a sacred object. It had been sawn out and made into a standard, carried before the cohort into many battles. It was battered now, scarred with arrow and spear marks. But that latrine had become a legend. Since they'd had it, the cohort had never lost a fight. It struck fear into even the fiercest of the painted people. Just the sight of it made them turn and run.

'Anyway,' said the other soldier, 'when Hadrian gets it, I hope that golden replica is as lucky for him as our standard has been for us.'

The legionaries limped away, moaning about blisters and all the extra duties they'd been lumbered with because of the royal visit.

But Superloo was ecstatic.

'So I'm right!' crowed the toilet in its quacky robot voice. Not that it had ever doubted it.

Using its giant computer brain, Superloo had done extensive research into toilet history. It had tapped into secret and long-forgotten files, unearthed every scrap of data. It had found hints, whispers, of the lucky latrine standard of the first cohort of the Fourth Legion. Most historians would say, 'Rubbish! It didn't exist.' But they'd swear blind, too, that Hadrian never came back to Britannica to see his Wall.

'*Cha!*' said Superloo scornfully. 'What do they know?'

Their human brains were feeble, compared to a toilet genius.

Pity those soldiers didn't come in, thought Superloo. It still needed two people to carry out its plan – to sneak into the fort and snatch the lucky latrine standard and the golden replica from right under the cohort's noses.

'Never mind,' Superloo consoled itself. 'There are plenty more humans where they came from.'

It slid open its door further and switched on its lights, to make the inside of its cubicle even more sparkly and welcoming.

CHAPTER THREE

Up at the fort, Scrofina slapped her servant girl hard across the face.

'You clumsy girl!' she screeched.

Scrofina was the wife of the fort commander. She was in a vile temper, as usual. Even brave and battle-scarred soldiers nicknamed her 'The Terror'. She'd had one of them flogged for saying she had a face like a ferret.

'You just stuck that hairpin into my head!' Scrofina twisted round and gave her another slap.

The servant girl didn't cry out. She knew better than to show any pain. She kept her face carefully blank. But behind her mistress's back, her eyes flashed defiance.

They were in the commander's house, the most luxurious place in the fort. And Scrofina's bedroom was grander still, with its fine furniture and mosaic floors. Noises drifted in from

13

outside. You could hear shouts, trumpets, clashing armour, as the cohort came back from patrol.

'How much longer will you take fixing my hair?' fumed Scrofina.

The servant girl peered at the gold Roman coin on the table, among the perfume bottles and make-up pots. It had a picture of the Emperor Hadrian's wife on it.

Scrofina had said, 'I want my hair just like hers! I don't want Hadrian to think I can't follow Roman fashions. Just because I'm stuck in this dump, surrounded by savages!'

Her own servant girl was one of those savages. Scrofina didn't know her name, or anything else about her. She probably came from one of those turf huts, hardly fit for pigs, that Scrofina saw from her litter when-ever she travelled outside the fort. She always tutted, 'How primitive,' and closed the curtains.

'You think you'd be grateful,' snapped Scrofina to her servant, 'to learn *civilized* Roman ways.'

The servant girl hid her scowl behind her long red hair. She was thirteen years old. She had a name – it was Briana. Briana's mum,

Birte, hadn't wanted her to work at the fort. They'd had terrific rows about it.

'I forbid you to wait on that Roman woman!' Birte had bawled, waving her sword about. 'You are a freeborn Brigantian princess!'

'So what?' Briana had yelled back, glaring round their smoky hut, with pigs running about. 'I'm still going! What kind of princess has to live like this?'

'Clear off then,' roared Birte, 'if we're not good enough for you!'

So Briana had stormed off to the fort, looking for something better. But she hadn't found it. She hated being a servant. And her new mistress was a nightmare. So would she make it up with her mum? Admit how miserable and homesick she was? No way. Just like Birte, Briana was proud and stubborn. She'd rather die than tell Mum, 'I made a mistake. You were right all along.'

Scrofina stared into a mirror. She puckered up her mean, pouty mouth. Eyes as hard and sour as acid drops stared back. Her lips and cheeks were stained crimson with berry juice. Her face was white chalky powder over a thick layer of bear's grease.

'*Humm*, lovely as ever,' she told herself.

She picked up a pair of gold dolphin earrings, then threw them down.

'You stupid girl, my hair's still wrong!'

On the coin, Hadrian's wife had an immense hair-do, like a curly-haired poodle squatting on top of her head.

'It's probably a wig, of course,' said Scrofina. A thought struck her. She stared at Briana's thick, red tresses, and stroked them between her fingers as if they belonged to her.

'Fetch the shears,' she ordered. 'Hadrian's coming the day after tomorrow. My wig-maker should just have time to do it.' Especially if she threatened him with a flogging.

'No, mistress,' said Briana, horrified, forgetting she must never answer back.

'You'll do what you're told!' snarled Scrofina, picking up a handy hairbrush to whack her with. 'That hair's wasted on you. And red hair's very fashionable in Rome. Fetch the shears.'

At that moment, an old slave came trembling in. 'Mistress, Nauseus the augur has arrived.'

Scrofina leapt up, scattering make-up pots. 'About time! That silly old fortune-teller better give me some straight answers!'

She flung an order over her shoulder at Briana, 'Go out and find me some more snails.' A mixture of crushed snails and honey was her favourite face cream. 'And be quick about it! I'll be chopping that hair off as soon as you get back.'

She bustled across the room, her gold bracelets clinking.

From the door, she rapped out another order: 'And no rubbish! Get me the best snails, from beyond the Wall.' Then she hurried away.

So much to do, she was thinking. She had to see Nauseus, then go down to the kitchen and screech at the servants to make sure they weren't slacking.

She'd planned a lavish banquet for Hadrian: larks' tongues, stuffed roasted dormice, all the things they ate in Rome. That was after the entertainment in the new amphitheatre, when a gladiator would be fighting a wild bear, captured from the forests beyond the Wall.

Hope they've starved that bear enough, thought Scrofina. She wanted a decent fight, with loads of blood.

She hadn't invited any local chiefs to the bear fight or the banquet afterwards. They were such yobs – always drinking, brawling, boasting and passing round their lucky heads during dinner, shouting, 'Mine's better than yours!' And that Birte was the worst of the lot. Scrofina shivered. The warrior queen had a fearsome reputation. She had heads hanging from her hut rafters like strings of onions.

'Oh no,' Scrofina had just remembered another problem. And it was nothing to do with Birte or Hadrian's visit.

Metellus, her husband, had been asking some awkward questions about Flaccus. Flaccus was Metellus's only child, his son from his first marriage. Flaccus's mum had died soon after giving birth to him. Metellus had quickly married Scrofina and, since he was away a lot, with his mind on military matters, he'd left the upbringing of his son to her. Scrofina couldn't be bothered with the baby. So she'd farmed him out to some relatives in faraway Tungria. That was thirteen years ago. On the rare occasions Metellus asked, Scrofina would say, 'Oh, Flaccus is happy. He's doing well at school.' But the truth was, she hadn't heard from those relatives for a very long time. She had no idea if the boy was dead or alive.

Stupid boy, thought Scrofina. *Why hadn't Flaccus died when he was a baby, along with his mum*? Now Metellus wanted to see him, as if he felt guilty for being such a distant father. He kept saying, 'It's time for my son's manhood ceremony. He should be here with us.'

Oh, bother the brat, thought Scrofina. She had no time to think about her stepson now. She had more important things on her mind. She hurried towards the courtyard.

Nauseus the augur was waiting for her. He was already shaking – he just knew he was in for a flogging. It was his job to tell the future by inspecting the guts of dead animals, watching how well the sacred chickens were feeding, and all sorts of other signs.

He looked the part, in his snowy white toga and silver circlet on his brow. But he was the worst augur in the whole Roman Empire.

Scrofina swept in as if she were the Empress herself. 'Right, you useless gut-gazer!' she snapped. 'I want some straight answers this time. Is the day after tomorrow a good day or not for Hadrian's visit? Are the sacred chickens feeding well? What do the guts tell you?'

'*Errr*,' said Nauseus, dithering, like he always did. 'I *think* the signs are auspicious. But I could be wrong,' he added, shrugging.

'I don't pay you to be wrong, you silly old fool!' screeched Scrofina, spitting mad. 'Can you predict the future or can't you?'

A voice chipped in. It was Nauseus's thirteen-year-old servant, the Keeper of the Sacred Chickens, coming to his master's rescue. Nauseus had bought him two years ago in a slave market. He was being sold cheap because he'd run away from his last master, who'd beaten him black and blue.

'My master is a great augur,' the Keeper of the Sacred Chickens assured Scrofina.

He didn't say, of course, that Nauseus hated the sight of blood. And if he looked at a pile of guts, would turn green and croak, 'How revolting! I think I'm going to throw up.'

Instead, the Keeper assured Scrofina, 'He is a very wise man, Mistress. He knows all the signs.'

That was a lie too. Nauseus was kind-hearted, miles better than the Keeper's last master. But he was so hopelessly vague and waffly. He was always getting the signs confused. Was a cawing raven a good or a bad omen? Was it bad luck when birds flew from right to left? Or should that be left to right? Nauseus could never remember.

Scrofina glared at the Keeper. He seemed far too bold and confident for a slave boy. He wasn't even cringing. 'How dare you address me?' she said. 'You should be whipped.'

Undaunted, the Keeper added, 'Back in Rome, all the ladies swear by him.'

That did the trick. Scrofina's biggest wish was to be like a Roman lady. She kept it secret that she'd never been to Rome. That she was a butcher's daughter, from Tungria. And she had caught Metellus's eye when he was marching through with his legion.

'Bring me those sacred chickens,' Scrofina commanded, in a slightly less scary voice. 'I want to see for myself how they are feeding.'

Whoops, thought the Keeper. *We're for it now*.

The truth was that the sacred cockerel had escaped that morning. If you listened, you could hear him, *cock-a-doodling* somewhere beyond the Wall. He was always doing a disappearing act. Whenever he did, his hens got all broody. They wouldn't feed until he came back. And if the sacred hens weren't feeding, that meant bad luck for Hadrian's visit. Something Scrofina definitely *didn't* want to hear, after all her preparations.

'*Errr*,' dithered Nauseus. '*Errr*.' He hitched

his toga over his shoulder and looked helpless.

Scrofina's eyes were flashing. That was a dangerous sign. She could have you flogged, or worse. Her husband, the Fort Commander, was an upright and decent Roman. When he was here, Scrofina had to behave. But Metellus was almost never at the fort – he was always out training his troops or fighting revolting natives.

Once again, the augur's quick-witted servant saved him.

'My lady,' said the Keeper. 'The sacred chickens are asleep now. But I will bring them to you the very moment they awaken.'

'Make sure you do,' snapped Scrofina. 'Now clear off! You've wasted enough of my time.'

'Don't you think she's just the *rudest* woman?' whispered Nauseus, as they bowed and scraped their way out of Scrofina's presence.

'I think I'd better find that sacred cockerel, and *quick*,' the Keeper whispered back.

Scrofina scowled – it was most annoying, not knowing if good fortune smiled on Hadrian's visit.

'It's too late to change it, anyway,' she said, out loud.

In the shadows, the red crest of a helmet

burned like fire. It was being worn by a tall, hawk-faced soldier. He'd been standing there, listening to everything. He clanked up to Scrofina. His arms were covered with scars from many campaigns.

'Clavus!' said Scrofina.

The Senior Centurion clashed his fist against his breastplate in salute. His armour was hung with the metal wreaths and medals he'd won. And the golden torcs he'd wrenched from the necks of the tribesmen he'd killed. Scrofina bullied servants. But she didn't dare bully Clavus.

'The signs are *not* auspicious for the day after tomorrow,' declared Clavus, fixing her with his cold, sinister stare.

'Oh,' said Scrofina. She didn't need to ask how he knew that. The god Mithras must have told him. Clavus and his centurion friends worshipped Mithras. They held secret ceremonies in his dark temple. Only the Brotherhood of Mithras could enter the temple; women and strangers weren't allowed. Especially now, when the replica golden latrine was stored in there, waiting for Hadrian's arrival.

'I shall send a signal,' said Clavus, 'telling the Emperor to arrive tomorrow instead. He could easily do it. By all reports, he's already at Carvoran.'

'Tomorrow?' shrieked Scrofina. 'But that's too soon! My wig isn't made yet! And has Sextus the Gladiator arrived?'

As she mentioned his name, the frosty Scrofina seemed to melt. Her eyelashes fluttered.

She simpered, 'He's come all the way from Rome. I'm just dying to meet him. They say he drives the ladies wild.'

She'd heard there was graffiti all over the walls of the Colosseum, scrawled by his adoring fans, like: *Suspirium puellarum Sextus* – Sextus makes the girls swoon.

'Sextus is here,' said Clavus. His granite face showed scorn. His lip curled in contempt. He muttered something under his breath. Was it, 'These pretty-boy gladiators wouldn't last two minutes in a real fight'? Everyone knew those fights in the Colosseum were fixed.

'But what about Metellus?' said Scrofina. 'He's taking out a patrol tomorrow. There are reports of trouble beyond the Wall.'

'We need not bother the Commander,' said Clavus, 'with these new plans. He has much on his mind. You and I can deal with Hadrian's visit on our own.'

Scrofina knew her husband should be told. She opened her mouth to say so, then closed it. Clavus wasn't a man you argued with.

She dared to ask, 'Will the Emperor heed your signal?'

'By Mithras, he'd better,' said Clavus grimly.

Even Hadrian would think twice before snubbing his senior centurions. Especially when they'd invited him to their fort, to give him a golden latrine. Plenty of times in the past, centurions had risen up, overthrown their Emperor and replaced him with one of themselves. And, by all accounts, Hadrian was paranoid about conspiracies. He'd even had some disguises made, different wigs, so he could mingle with the common people, unrecognized, and sniff out plots against him.

'If Mithras wills it,' said Scrofina, sounding strangely agreeable, 'the ceremony should certainly be brought forward.'

She'd suddenly seen the good side of these new arrangements. With Metellus out with his troops, she'd be the centre of attention at the banquet.

I'll have the Emperor all to myself, she thought.

She rushed off, her head spinning with all the servants she'd have to screech at to get things ready in time. 'I bet those cooks haven't stuffed the dormice yet! And that girl had better hurry back. I need her hair NOW!'

The Keeper scurried towards the North Gate of the fort. He paused only to watch the standard bearer, in his bearskin cloak, carry the cohort's lucky latrine standard into the Headquarters building. It would stay there, under guard, in the fort chapel, until it was needed for the next campaign.

Secretly, the Keeper clenched his fist, and gave his own soldier's salute. It was his dearest wish to join the army, even one day to be a centurion. But how could he, a mere slave? It was never going to happen.

He ran past the new amphitheatre, built especially for the Emperor's visit. It was inside the fort but away from the main buildings, so no one could hear the screams. Then he went through the ox carts and the crush of traders at the North Gate having their bags searched for weapons. He crashed into a tall man, wrapped in a grey cloak, waiting in the queue to come in. The Keeper was already yelling, 'Mind out!' as they collided. He thought the guy would go flying – he was an old geezer, judging by his masses of snowy-white hair. But instead, the Keeper bounced off the man's body, as if it was a tree trunk.

He picked himself up and ran on, into the scrubland that lay between the Wall and the dark forests beyond. It flashed through his mind, *What's that old guy wearing under that cloak?* Then he forgot about him. He had a sacred cockerel to catch.

As the Keeper ran, his long fair hair blew back from his forehead. You could see the letters FUG burned into his flesh. They stood for *Fugitivus*, Fugitive. They'd been branded there after he'd tried to escape from his last master. That was another reason why he could never become a soldier. Sometimes they accepted slaves. But slaves with 'FUG' on their foreheads?

'It's an impossible dream,' the Keeper told himself sternly. So why was he always tormenting himself with it?

Briana was already beyond the Wall, walking through heather, on springy moss. There were jagged grey rocks scattered everywhere, with snails jammed in their crevices. She was supposed to be collecting the biggest, juiciest ones to make face cream for Scrofina. But she'd got only two in her basket so far. She had other things on her mind. 'When I get back, Mistress will chop off all my hair.' It made her feel sick just to think of it.

And then Briana saw, ahead of her, something glittering in a grove of trees.

She crept closer, pushing her way through spiky gorse.

'What is it?' Her mouth fell open in wonder. Some kind of shrine? Someone must have built it just recently. It had never been here before.

She was dazzled by its sheen. There were shrines all over the countryside, to different deities. But she'd never seen one so splendid, nor one made all of silver. A very powerful spirit must live here.

She crept closer still and peeped in at the open door.

She saw a silver bowl, with water sparkling in it. 'A sacred pool!' she whispered. This must be the home of some kind of water god.

A cockerel crowed, just outside, but she was so entranced she scarcely noticed. She fell to her knees, clasped her hands. 'O divinity of this place, help me, or Scrofina will cut off my hair!'

She fumbled in her leather purse for a coin. It wasn't gold or silver, just a copper quadrans. But she threw it into the pool as an offering.

The pool gurgled. And, with a *whoosh*, whisked her coin away. The water god had accepted her humble gift!

Suddenly, the peace of the shrine was shattered. A boy came bursting in, scratched and bloody. He had a cockerel by the throat! He seemed to be wrestling with it. It beat at him with its wings, pecking him viciously. He had to let it go. It shot out of the shrine door in a great glitter of green and purple feathers.

'Curse that bird!' the boy cried. Briana thought, *I know him*. She'd seen him often, back at the fort.

The boy gazed around and seemed to realize he was in a sacred place. He, too, fell to his knees.

'Help me, O spirit of this place,' he begged. 'I must find that sacred cockerel, or the hens won't feed. And Scrofina will have my master whipped. And turn us out of the fort.'

And if they were thrown out of the fort, where would they go? There was only wilderness beyond the Wall.

For a brief time there was silence. The silver

walls sparkled. The water in the sacred pool swirled.

Then a voice boomed from the ceiling. '*Salvete!* Welcome, humans!' it said, echoing round the shrine.

'The spirit of the sacred pool *speaks!*' said the Keeper, his whole body quaking in terror.

'I will deal with the evil Scrofina,' thundered the water god. 'You need fear her no more. But you must do something for ME first. I seek the lucky latrine standard and its golden replica. Bring them *both* here to me, now.'

The Keeper and Briana stared at each other, dismayed. Did the water god know what he was asking? The task was a suicide mission. The standard was in the fort chapel – it was guarded twenty-four seven. Its golden copy was in the Temple of Mithras. Both places were off limits to most people, especially a slave and a servant girl. And everyone knew what had happened to the last slave who'd tried to steal the lucky latrine standard. He'd been sent to Rome in chains and fed to the lions.

'Will you undertake this task?' boomed the divinity.

The Keeper swallowed once, twice. Briana

looked pale. But did they have a choice? Gods got angry if you didn't obey. Their vengeance could be swift and terrible. Besides, this one *had* promised to deal with Scrofina. Perhaps zap her with a lightning bolt so she was just a heap of ashes.

But the Keeper had to ask one question. He didn't much care about the golden latrine but the lucky standard was another matter. It had brought the cohort victory in many battles. Still shaking in his sandals, he blurted out, 'But Divinity, you won't take the standard away, will you?'

The water in the sacred pool hissed, like hot, spitting fat. The god's voice swelled to a mighty roar that shook the shrine walls. 'How dare you,' the god thundered, 'a mere human, question MY actions!'

'Sorry, Divinity, sorry,' the Keeper trembled, hastily bowing his head. 'We are your servants. We hear and obey.'

CHAPTER FOUR

Finn was standing at the edge of a round, superloo-sized hole. He peered dizzily in. He was surprised by how deep it was. He could see cables down at the bottom, where Superloo had disconnected itself from its electricity supply. When it went into the past, it used power from its storage batteries to fuel its massive computer brain.

He'd been hanging around, waiting, for ages, for Superloo to come back.

He was getting worried. Superloo shouldn't be allowed out on its own. It was a super-intelligent toilet. But it had serious character flaws. When it came to its toilet ancestors, its brains went out of the window. It would do anything to get its hands on them: cheat, bully, tell you lies.

'I assume,' said a voice behind him, 'it'll *have*

to return soon to re-charge its storage batteries. How long before they run out? I'd say forty-eight hours. Maybe more. Maybe less.'

Finn whirled around. A little old man had come out of the weedy wasteland. He had alert blue eyes. He was wearing a duffel coat.

'How do you know that?' gasped Finn. 'About the storage batteries?' He'd thought he was Superloo's only friend.

'Because I know everything there is to know about toilets. I am the world's leading toilet expert,' answered the little old man. There was no hint of boasting in his voice. It was just a fact. 'I am Lew Brush,' he introduced himself. 'Caretaker of the Toilet Museum.'

'Toilet Museum?' said Finn, still in a daze. Like everyone else, he had no idea his town *had* a toilet museum.

'Yes, it's behind the Hi-Tech Toilet factory, the firm that made this most interesting toilet and fitted the wrong microchip in it by mistake.' Mr Lew Brush shook his head in wonder. 'I thought I'd seen almost every type of toilet. But I have never come across a toilet with a mind of its own.'

'Or a toilet that can time-travel,' Finn burst out. Maybe he shouldn't have said that. But

33

he couldn't help himself. This guy thought he knew everything about Superloo. Well, he was wrong.

Mr Brush felt an electric thrill running through his body. This just got better and better. He hadn't felt so excited since he got that glow-in-the-dark toilet seat for his collection – the one that helped you aim straight without having to switch on the bathroom light.

'I guessed that's what it was up to,' said Mr Lew Brush, 'when I saw you coming out of it in Ancient Egyptian clothes.'

'You saw me?' said Finn.

Then he noticed the binoculars round Mr Brush's neck. How long had this guy been spying on him and Superloo? That last trip to King Tut's tomb was days ago.

'This is all so fascinating,' said Mr Lew Brush. 'This toilet is unique.'

'Oh, and it can talk too,' added Finn, as if that was a minor detail.

'Bliss!' said Mr Brush, clasping his hands together.

He could hardly believe it. A toilet that thought for itself? A toilet you could talk to? Even have an intelligent conversation with?

'I've been waiting all my life for this,' Mr Lew Brush told Finn. 'It's like a dream come true!'

Then Mr Lew Brush shook his head and frowned. He mustn't get carried away. The truth was, he could talk about toilets for hours. It wasn't just his hobby, it was his lifelong passion. But there were more urgent things to attend to.

'Look, none of that matters at the moment,' he said briskly. 'What matters is, Superloo is in danger. And you and I have got to protect it.'

'In danger?' said Finn. 'Who from?'

'There are people out there,' said Mr Lew Brush, 'who want to find it and terminate it. It's that microchip – the Managing Director of Hi-Tech Toilets told me all about it. It shouldn't be in a toilet at all. It's part of a multi-billion-dollar space-research programme to make rockets speed through light years in seconds. My guess is that it somehow got put into Superloo the wrong way round, so it travels backwards through time instead of forwards . . .'

Finn had stopped listening at *terminate*. 'Terminate? You mean they want to *kill* Superloo?'

'Exactly,' said the Toilet Museum Caretaker, his face grim. 'They're hunting it now. Special Forces are on their way. They want to take out the microchip, shut down that brilliant brain. We mustn't let them do it.'

'No way!' said Finn. 'That would be murder!'

Mr Brush usually had no time for children. But he could see that he and this kid could work together – they were on the same wavelength.

'I totally agree,' he told Finn. 'It would be a terrible crime.'

Finn's head whipped round. 'What's that noise?'

From among the weeds and derelict buildings came a desolate howl.

'What on earth is it?' Finn whispered, the hairs prickling on the back of his neck. There it was again. 'Owwww! Owwww!' It sounded so mournful, so desperately hopeless.

'Oh, that,' said Mr Brush, who didn't seem at all bothered. 'That's just my bloodhound, Blaster. He always does that if he thinks he's lost me. I'm here, boy!' Mr Brush called out. 'Over here!'

A scabby nose poked out of the grasses,

followed by an anxious, baggy face. But when it saw Mr Brush, it gave shrill yaps of joy. The faithful old hound came shambling over. It hated being parted from its master, even for a minute. It thought it had been abandoned forever.

'Say hello to Finn,' said Mr Brush.

Uggh, thought Finn, as the decrepit old dog slobbered over his hand.

'*Jud jud jud jud.*'

Finn's gaze flew up to the skies.

A helicopter was hovering over the disused industrial estate.

'It's them,' said Mr Lew Brush. 'The Special Forces.'

'*JUD JUD JUD.*'

The throbbing sound grew deafening.

The 'copter swooped lower, its rotor blades starting a mini-hurricane, making the tree tops toss wildly about.

Then the world went really crazy. A rope snaked out from the hovering 'copter. Men in commando gear came swarming down. As Finn and Mr Brush gazed, open-mouthed, there was a whirring noise and a thud behind them.

Finn spun round. 'Superloo! You've come home!'

What had happened to the time-travelling toilet? Its sleek silver sides were dented and battered. It door slid wonkily open.

'Quick,' said Mr Lew Brush, 'before we're seen.'

Finn dived in at the open door and Mr Brush dragged Blaster inside.

The door slid shut. It was pitch black in here – why hadn't Superloo switched on its cubicle lights? Finn felt his stomach give a sick lurch, as if he was plunging down in a lift.

From somewhere came a loud tooting sound and a rather foul smell.

'That wasn't me,' said Mr Brush. 'It was Blaster – it happens when he gets nervous.'

'What's going on?' cried Finn.

Mr Brush's voice came again out of the dark. It sounded quite calm, in the circumstances. 'Superloo's retracting,' said Mr Brush. 'Going underground.'

'I didn't know it could do that,' said Finn.

Another voice joined in. 'I am *here*, you know!' It was Superloo's pompous robot tones. 'Yes, it is one of my many talents,' it told Finn. 'I am what is vulgarly known as a pop-up loo.'

'I didn't know that,' Finn repeated, sounding

hurt, as if Superloo had kept a secret from him.

'*Cha!*' said Superloo, with that familiar scornful snort. 'I can do many things you don't know about.'

It sounded like its usual smug, snooty self. But Finn knew something about Superloo by now: it had a vulnerable side, behind that giant ego. And he could detect, under its boasting and bluster, a little tremble in its voice.

Finn knew he was right when, from its audio system, a few bars of 'Drip, drip, drop little April showers' came floating out. Superloo had many tunes stored in its computer brain that it had downloaded (quite legally) from the Net. But this was its favourite. It played it in stressful times to soothe and reassure itself, like a toddler stroking a comfort blanket.

'What have you been up to?' demanded Finn, like a suspicious parent. 'And, by the way, have you got any of that lemony pine scent left you use for cleaning? It pongs a bit in here.'

Superloo deliberately ignored him. It had re-connected itself to its electricity supply. Now its cubicle lights came blazing on at full power.

'Who is this human with you?' demanded Superloo.

'I am Mr Lew Brush, Curator of the famous Toilet Museum,' Mr Brush introduced himself. 'And I am honoured to make your acquaintance.'

'Charmed, I'm sure,' the toilet replied.

'I am,' said Mr Brush modestly, 'something of a toilet expert. In fact, you could say, my whole life is toilets. Especially ancient toilets.'

'Ancient toilets?' cried Superloo, like an excited little kid. 'Wow! In that case, I'm over the moon to meet you!'

It had at last found a human who wasn't as dumb as the others, one who took toilets seriously. And obviously appreciated toilet history! It couldn't wait to chat. 'I'm in the middle of rescuing *two* ancient toilets,' it told Mr Lew Brush. 'I'm off to finish the job as soon as I've recharged. One is the lucky latrine standard of the first cohort of the Fourth Legion. The very latrine Hadrian sat on when he had the idea of his Wall. And the other is its golden replica, that's just about to be presented to him by loyal legionaries.'

'But this is wonderful news!' said Mr Brush. 'I can hardly believe it!'

'I know!' gushed the toilet. 'Neither could I!'

'And you say you've almost obtained them?'

'I'm *soooo* close,' said Superloo.

'Look, I hate to interrupt,' Finn chipped in. He'd been gazing round the cubicle in stunned silence. 'But what happened here?'

Superloo's cubicle was usually spotless. The stainless-steel toilet bowl, the big digital clock, the mirror, the jumbo bog-roll holder and automatic hand-washing facility – everything was sleek, sparkling and sanitized. But now it was just a shambles.

There were coins and other stuff in the toilet bowl. And hung everywhere, like Christmas tree decorations, were strange little charms, made of clay and metal.

'What are these?' asked Finn, looking closer. Then he answered his own question. 'They're little models of arms and legs! Of bits of people's bodies!' He looked closer still. What was that body bit? 'For heaven's sake,' said Finn, 'that's a bit rude.'

He blushed bright red in embarrassment and looked away.

He asked Superloo, 'Where do these come from?'

'Oh,' said Superloo off-handedly, 'back in Roman Britain they thought I was a god. They left offerings of coins. And models of the sick bits of their bodies, so I could heal them.'

'A god?' repeated Finn, astonished.

'So?' said Superloo, as if being worshipped didn't surprise it at all.

But Finn smelled a rat. Superloo wasn't telling the whole truth. 'Why did you come back,' he challenged it, 'without those ancient toilets?' He knew Superloo would risk anything, even running low on power, rather than return without its toilet relatives. 'It wasn't just to re-charge, was it?'

Superloo said nothing.

'I'm waiting,' said Finn. Usually the toilet was a terrible chatterbox. When it clammed up, you knew it had something to hide.

Suddenly Superloo crumbled; its voice dissolved into sobs. 'Everything went pear-shaped,' it whimpered. 'It wasn't my fault, honest it wasn't. They've been shut up in prison. They're being thrown to a bear in the amphitheatre tomorrow.'

'Thrown to a bear?' said Finn, horrified. 'Who are?'

'The slave boy, the one they call Keeper, and the servant girl Briana. I commanded them to bring me the ancient latrines. But they both got caught and . . .'

Finn was still confused. But he'd got the gist. 'Do you mean that, back in Roman Britain, two kids have been sentenced to death because of you?' he asked, outraged. 'To be *eaten alive* by a bear?'

'That makes it sound really bad,' snivelled Superloo. 'I admit I left a bit of a mess behind.'

'*A bit of a mess!*' yelled Finn. 'That's an understatement! You've got to go back, straight away, and sort it all out.'

'I agree,' said Mr Brush. 'And if you can get hold of those two ancient toilets at the same time, that would be great.'

'Who cares about two smelly old loos!' raved Finn. Were these toilet fanatics completely out of touch with reality? 'Two kids are about to die a horrible death,' he reminded them.

Mr Brush had the grace to look ashamed.

'Will you come with me, Finn?' quavered Superloo. 'I need your help. I really do.'

Oh no, thought Finn. *So that's what it came back for.*

But he couldn't help feeling flattered. Superloo had asked him, personally, for help. For such a proud and intelligent toilet, that must have been hard.

It was against his better judgement, and warning bells were clanging in his head. But, despite all that, Finn heard himself saying, 'All right, I'll come.' He turned to Mr Lew Brush. 'Are you coming too?' he asked him.

'No,' declared Mr Brush. Suddenly he was all efficiency. His blue eyes sparkled with fighting spirit. He didn't pull any punches.

'You're being hunted,' he told Superloo. 'By specially trained troops. And if they find you they'll terminate you. They don't want that microchip brain of yours to fall into the wrong hands.'

'I know,' said Superloo, who'd tapped into all the secret communications being sent from the Special Forces to the Managing Director of Hi-Tech Toilets.

'OK then,' said Mr Lew Brush. 'So I'll stay here and create a diversion. Keep them away from where you live.'

Anyone who knew anything at all about toilets would only have to glance into this hole to know it belonged to a pop-up public convenience.

'Can you really do that?' asked Superloo.

'Oh yes,' said Mr Brush. 'I was an under-cover agent during the war, working behind enemy lines. I haven't forgotten all my old spying tricks.'

'Thank you,' said Superloo, for once sounding genuinely grateful.

'I'll be off then,' said Mr Brush.

With a *whoosh* Superloo shot up from its underground den. It opened its door, just a tiny bit.

Mr Brush sneaked a look outside. 'All clear,' he said.

The helicopter had gone and there was no sign of the soldiers who'd abseiled down from it. But they wouldn't be far away.

'Bye,' said Mr Brush. 'Just leave the twenty-first century to me. Come on, Blaster.'

The crumbling old hound tottered out after his master.

'Wait a minute,' said Finn. 'I haven't got the right clothes.' He was wearing his usual jeans and T-shirt. He'd stick out like a sore thumb in Roman Britain.

'Here,' said Mr Brush. He shrugged off his coat. 'This'll do.'

'I'm not wearing that!' said Finn. 'It's a duffel coat!'

'It's perfect,' said Superloo. 'It looks a bit like a *Birrus Britannicus*.'

45

'A what?' said Finn.

'A sort of hairy hooded garment, made of goatskin, that was all the rage back in Roman Britain. Did it have sleeves?' mused Superloo. 'Or was it more cloak-like? Historians disagree . . .'

'Look,' interrupted Finn. 'Aren't we wasting time?'

'Anyway,' said Superloo, 'it had a hood, that's certain. And it fastened with a big brooch . . .'

'I'm not wearing a big brooch,' warned Finn. 'So don't ask me. Anyway, I've got toggles.'

Gingerly, Finn put on the duffel coat. It was rough and shaggy and miles too big. It smelled like old dog.

'OK,' said Finn, fastening his toggles. 'Shouldn't we be going now?' He was thinking about those poor kids, sentenced to death.

Superloo's door began sliding shut. 'One last thing,' said Mr Brush, poking his head back in. 'Could you possibly bring me back an authentic Roman bottom-wiping sponge? I've always wanted one.'

With a click the door closed.

'Disengage electricity,' quacked Superloo. 'Switch power to storage batteries.' They were about to take off.

'I meant to ask,' said Finn. 'What are those marks on your outside? Those dents? Like you were attacked, with a big sword or something?'

'I was!' said Superloo. 'By Birte. That woman's a maniac!'

'Who's Birte?' said Finn. 'I don't understand.'

'I'll fill you in on the details when we get there. Are you ready?'

As I'll ever be, thought Finn, hanging on to the toilet bowl. Then he said, 'Wait a minute. There's something in the water.'

'I told you,' said Superloo. 'People chucked in coins. They thought I was a water god and that was my sacred pool.'

'No, besides the coins.' Finn gritted his teeth and plunged his hand into the toilet bowl. He groped round the U-bend.

'Here it is,' he said, shaking the water off. It was a small, thin sheet of metal. 'There's writing scratched on it,' said Finn.

'Sounds like a curse tablet,' said Superloo, who had everything there was to know about Roman history stored in its vast data banks. 'It's in Latin, I suppose? Just read out the words, I'll translate.'

As Finn stumbled over the strange language, Superloo said, 'That doesn't make sense even to me. I think it's some kind of code.' Its computer brain whirred. 'I've cracked it!' it said, triumphantly, after 2.5 seconds. 'It's the code the Brotherhood of Mithras used to send secret messages to each other.'

'So what's it say?' asked Finn.

'It says, "*Great Water God*". That's ME,' explained Superloo smugly. '"*Let Hadrian fall under our swords at the banquet. Let him be hacked to bits and Clavus made Emperor in his place. And if Metellus tries to stop us let him too feel the sharpness of our daggers.*" Oh dear,' said Superloo. 'That's not very nice, is it? I think it's a conspiracy.'

'What?' said Finn. He was thoroughly confused and he hadn't even left the twenty-first century.

'It means they're plotting to kill Hadrian, at the banquet after the latrine presentation ceremony.'

'Kill Hadrian?' said Finn, shocked. 'We've got to stop them!'

'Well, I suppose he *was* one of the better Roman Emperors,' said Superloo. 'Although that's not saying much.'

'So who threw this curse tablet in there?'

asked Finn.

'I'm not sure,' admitted Superloo.

As it waited for Briana and the Keeper to come back with the latrines, so many people had come calling. They'd all wanted something from the water god – miracle cures or loads of cash, or nasty things done to their neighbours.

'Just try to remember,' said Finn. 'It's important.'

Superloo zipped through its memory files. Its sensors had given it masses of data about each visitor: height, weight, whether they were male or female and a hundred other details. It hadn't even needed this kind of detection. People tell gods all sorts of things. Just by listening, Superloo had learned a lot: people's hopes and fears, all the local gossip.

For instance, most of the girls had a crush on the same guy. 'Oh please, Divinity,' they'd begged, 'make Sextus look in my direction. Make him fall madly in love with me!'

But one visitor hadn't asked for anything. He'd been silent, except for the jingling of his armour, the clanking of his sword.

'I've got it!' crowed Superloo. 'It was a soldier who left it. A centurion.'

He'd had a vine stick; it had tapped on the floor. And Superloo's auditory sensors in the ceiling, sharper than a bat's ears, had detected the breeze ruffling his helmet crest.

'You mean some of his own centurions are plotting to kill the Emperor?'

'Happened all the time in Ancient Rome,' said Superloo.

'And maybe kill someone called Metellus too?' said Finn.

'Pity about him,' said Superloo. 'According to what I heard, he's a good Fort Commander.'

'So shouldn't we *do* something?'

'Well, it's not my fault, the conspiracy thing,' Superloo pointed out.

'Yeah, but it's your fault those kids are going to be eaten by a bear!'

Superloo felt a strange, unfamiliar sensation fizzing deep in its circuits. Was it guilt? It was remembering how it had found out what had happened to the Keeper and Briana. Two visitors had told him. One was Nauseus the augur. He'd come rushing into the cubicle. Superloo detected his toga flapping around him, like the wings of a big bird.

He'd just gone to pieces. 'Help me, Divinity,' he'd pleaded pathetically. 'The Keeper isn't just my slave. He's a friend. I don't know what I'm going to do without him.' Then he'd collapsed in a heap and wept buckets. Superloo's floor sensors had been drenched.

The other visitor had been quite different. She hadn't come to plead; she didn't want help. She wanted vengeance!

'Call yourself a divinity!' she'd roared. 'Sending innocent girls to steal standards, get themselves captured? You ought to be ashamed of yourself.'

And she'd set about Superloo with her huge broad sword. *Clang!* 'Take that!' *Clang!* Superloo had closed its doors to keep her out. So she'd smashed up the outside instead.

'Let's get going,' said Finn impatiently, breaking into Superloo's thoughts. 'We've got at least three people's lives to save.'

Someone hammered on the cubicle door. It was Mr Lew Brush. 'What are you waiting for?'

He could see the tops of the tall grasses moving, clouds of pollen shaken off. Were the toilet hunters creeping through it, coming this way?

But inside, Superloo was at last getting a move on. 'Blast off!' it cried.

As its lights flashed, its cubicle began to

rotate, slowly at first, then it picked up speed.

Suddenly, the world dissolved into a silver cyclone. Finn clung on grimly. But as Superloo spun back through the centuries, he felt his fingers slipping. 'Oh no!'

Wham! He was whisked away from the toilet bowl and spreadeagled against the wall. The centrifugal force kept him stuck there, hung up like a picture.

After the last trip he should have been used to it. But he wasn't. 'I feel sick,' wailed Finn, as Superloo whirled faster and faster. Tiny charms of arms and legs and other, unmentionable, body bits twirled around too, in a crazy dance.

Outside, as soon as Superloo vanished, Mr Lew Brush sprang into action. Puffing and panting, his creaky old knees protesting, he lifted up a rusty sheet of corrugated iron. Woodlice scuttled in all directions. Using all his strength, he dragged it over Superloo's underground den. His faithful bloodhood, Blaster, tried to help by gripping the sheet with his few wobbly teeth, but he collapsed in a wheezing heap after the first tug.

'It's all right, boy, you have a rest, I'll handle

this,' said Mr Brush.

All around the grass was rippling. These guys were experts, silent as Native American trackers. They didn't even crack a twig.

But Mr Brush wasn't deterred. He'd already formed a bond with the super-intelligent toilet. It shared his passion for ancient loos for a start. And it was going to bring him back an authentic Roman bum-wiping sponge! For that prize alone, he would defend Superloo to his last breath.

Clang! The metal sheet dropped into place. Just in time. The blunt nose of a machine gun parted the weeds. A voice rapped, 'Don't move! We've got you surrounded.'

'Don't shoot,' quavered Mr Lew Brush, raising his hands in the air. 'Don't shoot. I'm just a harmless old man.'

CHAPTER FIVE

Finn felt a jarring shock. Superloo had spun to a stop. There was a thump as it landed that rattled Finn's teeth. He came unstuck from the wall and slid in a heap on the floor. Charms fluttered around him like dead leaves. He staggered dizzily to his feet.

'We've arrived in Roman Britain,' said Superloo. 'At dawn on the day *before* Hadrian arrives for the lucky latrine ceremony. If I'm not mistaken, the presentation will be tomorrow afternoon, followed by the entertainment in the amphitheatre, then the banquet.'

'Entertainment!' said Finn, aghast. 'Kids being torn to bits by a bear?'

'Anyway, we've got plenty of time to sort things out,' said Superloo breezily, ignoring Finn's outburst.

But Superloo didn't know everything. It

didn't know yet that the ceremony had been brought forward, so that Clavus and his Brotherhood of Mithras mates could kill Hadrian while Metellus and the cohort were out on patrol.

'But I can't be gone until tomorrow!' Finn was protesting. 'My mum'll have kittens if I don't turn up for tea.'

'*Cha!*' said Superloo contemptuously. 'Haven't you grasped this time-travel thing yet? Times in the past and present do not relate. Whatever happens, you'll be back in the twenty-first century well before teatime on the same day you left.'

Finn sighed. He could feel a headache coming on. 'It's all very complicated.'

'Never mind,' said Superloo. 'Don't trouble your poor human brain about it. Just trust me.'

Finn frowned. Trusting Superloo wasn't that easy. He'd had too much experience of its wily ways, how it manipulated humans for its own ends.

Superloo had been aiming for the same grove of trees it had landed in last time. But it couldn't detect any birdsong outside or rustle of leaves.

'I might have made a slight miscalculation,'

it admitted. 'I'll just open the door and you can find out exactly where we are.'

'No!' said Finn, suddenly overcome with panic at what might be waiting out there. 'Not yet. I'm not ready. There's some questions I want to ask first.'

Only metres away, the Keeper and Briana were huddled in a grim little cell. It had been dug under the new amphitheatre. Around them were other underground cells. They seemed empty but it was hard to be sure. A grey light came from outside, down the sloping tunnel that led to the arena. But it hardly made any difference to the murky darkness.

Just now, they'd heard a *thud* and thought they'd seen a gleam far back in the shadows. But then everything had gone quiet again and the Keeper had said, 'We imagined it.'

Now they were talking in low, scared whispers.

'What's all this sand for?' said Briana.

Great bags of sand were stacked with them in their cell. They were sitting on the sacks.

The Keeper couldn't tell her the truth: that the sand was for soaking up blood in the arena. Between every contest, a fresh lot would be scattered.

Instead the Keeper said, 'Don't think about what's happening tomorrow.' His own stomach churned as he said it. Since they'd met in the shrine, he'd learned something she hadn't. That the ceremony was taking place today. He thought, *You should tell her. But not yet. Let her think they have plenty of time.*

'You don't seem very scared,' said the Keeper.

'That's because I'm sure the water god will help us,' said Briana. 'He promised to protect us.'

The Keeper wished he had her faith. Privately, he thought he'd been a fool to rush off on some hopeless errand just because some water god ordered him to. Who was he anyway? He didn't even have a name. He was probably a very minor divinity with hardly any powers. And, even if he did have powers, why should he help them, since they'd both failed in the tasks he'd set them?

'I *almost* got the golden latrine,' the Keeper told Briana. 'I could *see* it, on the altar, under the picture of Mithras slaying the bull.'

Yesterday, he'd gone sneaking towards the temple, his heart racing. He knew even being in there was forbidden, let alone trying to snatch the golden latrine that was meant for Hadrian.

He'd had to dodge back behind a pillar as two centurions came out.

'The signal has already been sent,' said one, 'to summon Hadrian here for the ceremony a day early.'

'Yes,' said the other, 'and the golden latrine won't be all he'll be getting.'

They both laughed unpleasantly. The Keeper couldn't make any sense of that.

He'd slid out from behind the column. His heart had almost stopped. There he was again – that mysterious stranger from the North Gate! The guy in the grey cloak, with the flowing white hair and the metal body. They'd almost collided again. Just who *was* he? He seemed to be everywhere. Had he heard those centurions talking? But he hadn't even glanced at the Keeper. He'd just wrapped his grey cloak around him, put up his hood and slipped away.

The Keeper had forgotten him – he'd had more important things on his mind. He'd just learned that the presentation was a day early. If he wanted to steal the golden latrine for the water god, this might be his only chance.

The temple of Mithras was only a tiny

building. But it was a spooky, cave-like place. The Keeper shivered; he could feel a frosty chill down his spine. There were benches along both sides but they were in shadow. Smoky oil lamps flickered on the altar. They lit up the gory mural above them: the god Mithras plunging his knife into a bull's neck and the blood squirting out like a fountain.

The Keeper had looked around, wondering, 'Where's that latrine?' His heart was thudding now, his mouth dry. The resiny perfume from smouldering pine cones caught in his throat, making his head swim.

Then he'd seen it, gleaming gold on the altar. An exact copy of the original, only smaller. He'd rushed towards it, desperate to grab it and escape. But then the shadows had come alive! Creatures had lunged at him from the benches and seized him. Monsters with men's bodies and ravens' heads! Then the one gripping his arm had pulled off his mask. And the Keeper had seen the brand of Mithras between his brows, recognized him as one of the fort centurions. The Brotherhood of Mithras had caught him red-handed.

Now Briana was telling him how she'd been captured. She'd got within sight of her latrine too. She just walked straight past the guards into the Headquarters building. No one had suspected her, a servant girl. Anyway, they'd thought she was on some errand for Scrofina.

'I got right to the chapel,' Briana said, 'and the lucky latrine standard was there. I reached out and touched it. But then a guard grabbed me. He said, "Not another native trying to nick our standard!" He dragged me in front of Scrofina. And she said, "I never trusted her. You try to be kind to these savages, and look what happens." She told him to lock me up and give her the key.'

'What did she want the key for?' asked the Keeper.

'She's going to come down here and cut off all my hair,' said Briana, her lip trembling. 'She wants a wig made out of it.'

The Keeper was horrified. In a few hours, they would be a wild bear's dinner. But, somehow, Briana losing her hair shocked him even more.

'You've got lovely hair!' he raved. 'I won't let her do it!'

But what could he do? He was helpless, locked up here in the amphitheatre, under sentence of death.

'What's that?' said Briana. She'd heard another sound from the darkness: a sniffle, a sort of snort. 'Is there something in here with us?' she said.

The Keeper said, 'I didn't hear anything.' He was trying his best to be brave, but Briana noticed he was clutching a charm that was round his neck.

'What's that?' she said. The Keeper showed her. Briana squinted in the gloom. It was a small painting of a woman, faded, almost rubbed out. But you could still see her dark hair and her smiling eyes. 'It *might* be my mother,' said the Keeper.

'Don't you know?' asked Briana.

He said, 'The people who brought me up once said it was. But they were cruel, they sold me into slavery, and they told my new master I had no parents, that I was an orphan. So I don't know.' The Keeper shrugged sadly. 'I don't know who I am, or where I came from.'

Briana said, 'I'm sorry.' She laid her hand on his. She and her own mum often screamed at each other. They were both strong, fiery people who wouldn't back down. *But at least,* thought Briana, *I've got a mum.*

Briana wondered if her mum knew where

61

she was. By now, the news of their arrest must be all over the fort. But had it spread yet to the native settlements?

The light coming down the tunnel changed from grey to pink. It must be dawn outside. Briana sniffed the air longingly. Could she smell the honey scent of the bright yellow gorse bushes beyond the fort? She thought she could.

'What's that?' The Keeper's head whipped round. He got off the sand sacks to look, clinging on to the bars. He peered into the shadows. This time he was sure he'd heard something.

'Somebody's snoring,' he whispered.

Snoring, snorts and sniffles, mysterious thuds and gleams of silver: they definitely weren't alone. In fact, there seemed to be a whole crowd of people in here with them!

Inside Superloo, Finn was still putting off the evil moment when he had to step outside.

'Wait!' he begged Superloo again. 'Remind me what's happened so far. Just get me up to speed!'

Finn could have sworn he heard Superloo take a deep, exasperated breath. But his ears must have been deceiving him. Superloo didn't have lungs, or a heart. It was just a microchip brain inside a public convenience.

It started talking. It had been talking for some time before Finn pleaded, 'Stop, stop.'

'What bit of what I've just said don't you understand?' asked Superloo in its most fussy, teacherish tones.

'Well, who all these people are for a start! Look, have I got this right? Metellus the Fort Commander – he's a good guy but he's never around. And Scrofina his wife, she's a bad person. And Briana's her servant girl, who's been condemned to die cos she was caught nicking the lucky latrine standard. And this Keeper kid, he's the slave of Nauseus, the useless augur, and he's going to die too . . .'

'You've forgotten Clavus, Senior Centurion, the leader of the plot to kill Hadrian,' sighed Superloo, as if it was teaching a particularly dumb student.

'Oh yeah.' It was a good job Finn didn't have to take a test on all this; he could already feel a headache coming on.

'You forgot about Birte too,' added Superloo.

'Not another one,' said Finn 'Who's she?'

'I *told* you,' said Superloo, clucking impatiently. 'She's the one who got mad at me, beat me up with a broadsword. She's Briana's mum, by the way.'

'I'm not surprised she got mad at you then! Considering her daughter's going to be scoffed by a wild bear tomorrow. And it's all your fault.'

Superloo ignored that outburst. It had felt guilty, for about two seconds, for the mess it had left behind. Now it had bounced back and was full of self-belief again.

'My super brain will work out a solution,' it assured Finn. 'Are you ready yet?'

'Ready as I'll ever be,' muttered Finn, as Superloo's door slid open. But still he hesitated. What was he going to face out there? He should have been thinking about the dangers. But he was thinking the wildest, silliest thoughts: *Wish I didn't have to wear this duffel coat. Bet I look like a prat.*

Then he put up the hood and felt differently. It was quite snuggly in there. It wrapped around him like a duvet, covered his head, disguised his face. It made him feel bolder somehow. Even the smell was friendly. He took a big sniff. It reminded him of Blaster and Mr Lew Brush, back home in the twenty-first century.

He swallowed hard, then, hidden deep inside his big smelly coat, Finn stepped outside.

And almost rushed straight back in. Superloo had dimmed its cubicle lights. But by their soft glow Finn had seen tiny dark rooms, tunnels – an underground labyrinth.

'*Hey,*' he whispered, horrified. 'We're not back in King Tut's tomb, are we?'

'*Cha!*' snorted Superloo scornfully. 'What do you take me for? My time calculations are not that far out!'

Its hearing sensors were busy detecting, analysing tiny sounds.

'Did I tell you I could analyse smells too?' it asked Finn.

'What?' frowned Finn.

'Yes, I have an E-nose, or Electronic Nose,' boasted Superloo. 'Meant for analysing the air quality in space rockets, sniffing out poisonous gases.'

'For heaven's sake!' hissed Finn. 'What's that got to do with anything? I want to know where we've landed!'

'But that's precisely what I'm telling you,' said Superloo in the voice it reserved for stupid humans. 'My E-nose detects the smell of geraniums – and pigeon dung.'

'Geraniums? Pigeon dung?' echoed Finn, bewildered.

'Yes,' lectured Superloo, as if it was giving a history lesson. 'A gladiator would dye his hair blond with pigeon dung and rub himself all over with scented oils, to make himself lovely for the Roman ladies. I think we've landed under the amphitheatre.'

Finn didn't hear any of that last bit. He'd stopped listening at the word 'gladiator'. He was panic-stricken now.

'I've heard about gladiators,' he hissed. 'I've seen films. They were really tough guys, rock hard. No *way* am I going out there!'

'It's OK,' said Superloo breezily, 'he's probably in chains. Most gladiators were slaves. This one's called Sextus – I forgot to tell you about him. He's going to fight the bear in the arena tomorrow, after it's eaten the Keeper and Briana.'

'Oh, great,' sighed Finn. Yet another thing he didn't know about. Now his shivering fit was even worse. He took a few wobbly steps outside. It was a good job he didn't hear Superloo saying behind him, 'Oh, by the way, I smell bear too.'

CHAPTER SIX

Finn could hardly see in the gloom. Superloo's lights cast a dim glow, but most of the place was in shadow. He saw beams holding up an earth roof, a wide tunnel, bars. Where was he? It looked like a prison.

'Ow! Ow! Ow!'

Finn whirled around. Those were cries of pain, he was sure of it. Was someone being horribly tortured? His heart racing, ready at any moment to sprint back to Superloo, he crept up to the nearest cell.

Phew, what's that flowery smell? thought Finn, as a waft of geraniums hit him. He peered in. There was a guy in there, sitting on a low wooden bed. He was huge and hunky, a giant of a man. His muscles glistened with oil. He had bleached blond hair that stuck up in spikes.

It must be Sextus the Gladiator, thought Finn.

But what was he doing? Finn could hardly believe his eyes. He had a tiny pair of tweezers. And he was pulling out his toe hairs, one by one. Finn winced. That must hurt.

'Ow!' said Sextus, as he moved on to his smooth, oily chest and ripped out a few stray hairs.

Finn just couldn't help it. There were some things you had to ask about. He dashed back to Superloo.

'Hey,' he whispered, 'you're not going to believe what I just saw. That Sextus is plucking his chest hair out. With tweezers.'

'Of course he is,' quacked Superloo, as if it wasn't at all surprised. 'He's going through his beauty routine. Roman ladies go for blond guys with smooth skins. They hate rough, hairy men. A gladiator has to look good for his lady fans.'

'Oh, right,' said Finn doubtfully. 'But isn't that a bit, well, cissy?'

He'd always thought gladiators were real he-men.

'It's not cissy, it's common sense,' said Superloo. 'It pays to stay popular with your fans. They can decide your fate in the arena. Thumbs up, you live; thumbs down, you die.'

'Oh, right,' said Finn, more thoughtfully.

'Look,' said Superloo. 'No more questions! We're here to save the Keeper and Briana. And don't forget about Hadrian.'

It carefully left out the two latrines. But it didn't plan to leave them behind. It had grown quite fond of Finn. And it had a new friend now – Mr Lew Brush. But, apart from those two, it cared about toilets more than humans.

'Sorry,' whispered Finn. It had slipped his mind for a second that at least three people were in desperate peril. 'I'll look in the rest of the cells. I'll do it right now.' He rushed off.

He tiptoed past Sextus. But he needn't have worried. The gladiator was busy scooping out his earwax with a little spoon.

He was muttering something, talking to himself. Finn didn't understand it. But Superloo did. 'This is the worst dressing room I've ever been in,' Sextus was grumbling. 'And this amphitheatre's just a joke. It's built out of mud. There's not even a band.'

Sextus was used to top venues like the Colosseum, where they put on really spectacular shows, with hundreds of wild beasts and gladiators. Where there was a huge crowd baying for blood and a band blasting out deafening, war-like music.

'Why did I come to this wet, foggy island? I should never have left Rome,' he moaned.

But the truth was that Sextus had been slipping in the ratings. Lately, his lady fans had been cheering for younger, better-looking guys. He was getting slow, too. So he'd been forced to try his luck in the provinces, where the gladiators were second rate, and the ladies weren't so picky.

You'll drive the ladies of Britannia wild, thought Sextus as he checked his looks in his bronze mirror. He didn't have much competition. The tribesmen round here seemed like rough, hairy brutes, not well groomed at all. If they were fighting a bear, like he was about to, you'd hardly be able to tell which was which.

Then Sextus frowned. He'd just caught sight of his ear in the mirror. It was clipped, showing he was a slave. He wasn't in chains, or even locked in – they trusted him not to run. But, after all these years fighting, he still wasn't a free man.

'At least you're fighting in front of the Emperor,' Sextus told himself. That cheered him up. And who'd have thought it, the

Emperor coming to this end-of-the-world place? Back in Rome, Sextus had fought in front of Hadrian many times. He'd always hoped that, after an especially good fight, the Emperor might have given him his freedom. But that had never happened.

Finn was sneaking past the gladiator's cell when he heard Sextus sigh and saw him stand up, tall and broad as an oak tree. Finn shrank back into the shadows.

Then, in a shaft of rosy light from outside, Finn saw him reaching his hand into the next cell. There was a shaggy heap hunched there. It growled softly. It turned and Finn saw a grey muzzle, two bewildered eyes.

It's the bear! thought Finn, freezing in terror.

'You must be hungry, my friend,' said Sextus. 'Never mind, you will have a meal soon.' He frowned. The bear had come from the wilderness beyond the Wall – had been trapped in the thick, dark forests. 'Were you the best they could catch?' said the gladiator, stroking the bear's rough coat.

It wouldn't be much of a contest. The bear was already thin, in poor condition. Sextus frowned to himself. Perhaps he was getting soft. But he just didn't want to fight the poor beast, although he knew he didn't have a choice.

'My friend,' said the gladiator, 'we're both captives, aren't we?' He wished both of them could be free. But that was an impossible dream.

Finn saw the bear snarl softly, show its yellow, snaggly teeth. He thought, *It's gonna rip his hand off!*

But it didn't. It just put out its pink tongue, licked Sextus's fingers.

Poor, mangy old thing, thought Finn. He forgot his fear. Instead, a wave of pity swept over him. It had such sad eyes. It reminded him of Blaster a bit, except not quite so decrepit. *I can't stand it*, thought Finn, *that poor creature locked up like that.*

He already had three people to save: Briana, the Keeper and Hadrian. But he added the bear to that list. He didn't know how he was going to set it free, but the determination burned like a fierce flame in his heart.

The bear hunched back into its corner. Sextus got busy again, looking in the mirror at his huge slab-like face, checking it for unsightly zits.

Finn moved on, peered into another cell.

'That must be them,' he breathed – the

Keeper of the Sacred Chickens and Briana.
They'd fallen asleep in each other's arms.

Awww, thought Finn. *How sweet.*

And then he remembered – they were
going to be thrown to the bear tomorrow –
it would be raging mad with hunger by then.
Even in its weak state, they wouldn't stand a
chance.

He took a closer look at them. Briana had
long, tumbling red hair. The boy had 'FUG'
on his forehead – was that his real name? *How
awful*, thought Finn, *branding a kid's name on his
forehead.* These Romans had some very cruel
customs.

'Fug, Briana, wake up,' Finn called softly
through the bars. 'Me and Superloo have come
to save you.'

The Keeper stirred.

In his excitement, Finn forgot he was
supposed to keep quiet, 'Hey!' he yelled back
to Superloo. 'I've found them!'

Several things happened at once. Superloo
flooded the cells and tunnel with a bright,
white glare. The Keeper's eyes shot open. The
bear, dazzled by the light, growled ferociously,
its mouth a red, gaping cave. And Sextus came
lumbering out of his dressing-room cell with

a three-pronged stabbing trident. He aimed it at Finn. 'Who are you, hooded intruder?' he roared. 'Identify yourself!'

He jabbed with the trident. Finn hurled himself to the floor and scuttled, crab-like, towards Superloo.

He didn't make it that far.

The trident streaked through the air and pinned his duffel-coat sleeve to the ground. He heard the thud of sandalled feet as Sextus charged after it.

Finn struggled to get free of his coat. Typical! The toggles wouldn't come undone! He saw five great hairless toes by his head. The trident was snatched back for another stab.

'Help me!' Finn screamed to Superloo, curling up into a ball.

Even brighter light, radiant as a heavenly beam, spilled from Superloo's door.

Everyone, even Sextus, covered their eyes.

The toilet spoke, in a voice like thunder.

'HOW DARE YOU TRY TO HARM MY SERVANT!'

The Keeper and Briana were at the bars now. 'It's the water god!' cried Briana. 'I knew he'd come to save us.'

Beside her, the Keeper stared, speechless. He'd never expected this. He'd made a big mistake about that divinity. It must be super-powerful, suddenly turning up here, under the amphitheatre, along with the shrine it lived in.

Sextus had fallen to his knees. He knew a god when he saw one. 'Forgive me, Divinity,' he bellowed.

Then Finn felt himself being lifted up, as if he weighed no more than a daisy. He was plonked back on to his feet. A shovel-sized hand dusted down his duffel coat.

Superloo knew it had made a big impact. Its circuits fizzed with satisfaction. It liked being a god; gods got maximum respect. As a toilet, even a super-intelligent one, all you got were sniggers and rude jokes.

'Right!' said Superloo, in Latin. 'Everyone listen to ME.'

Finn wasn't sure what Superloo was saying. But he knew those imperious tones. That toilet just loved being in charge.

'We have much to do before the latrine presentation ceremony tomorrow . . .' it began.

'May I speak, Divinity?' asked the Keeper from behind the bars of his cell.

'Make it quick,' snapped Superloo, annoyed at being interrupted.

'Divinity,' said the Keeper, 'the ceremony has been brought forward. It is to take place this afternoon. I heard two centurions talking outside the Temple of Mithras.'

Briana looked at the Keeper in horror. 'You didn't tell me that!' The colour drained from her face. She clung to the cell bars so she wouldn't collapse. She gazed hungrily at the tiny square of pink light at the distant tunnel entrance. Would this be the last dawn she and the Keeper saw?

'Help us get out of here, Divinity,' she begged. 'Scrofina has the key.'

Finn felt left out. 'What is everyone saying?' he asked.

Superloo gave him the gist.

'I'll go and get that key,' said Finn impulsively. He'd need someone to show him where to find Scrofina.

But Superloo was there ahead of Finn. 'Gladiator,' it commanded.

'Yes, Divinity!' Sextus thumped his fist across his chest.

'You must go with my servant. You have two important tasks. Get the key from Scrofina –

I want these two prisoners released. And find Metellus the Fort Commander. I have news to tell him. Clavus and his friends plan to kill Hadrian today, at the banquet, after the entertainment in the amphitheatre.'

'Murder my Emperor!' roared Sextus, who was fiercely loyal, even though Hadrian had never done *him* any favours.

'But Metellus is going out on patrol this morning,' the quick-thinking Keeper pointed out. 'He must have been kept in the dark about this change of plan. I think Clavus wants him and the cohort out of the way.'

'Then you must hurry,' Superloo told Sextus. 'Find Metellus before he leaves the fort. Bring him here to me.'

Sextus was a gladiator. But he was also a slave. If a slave told the Fort Commander that Clavus, his most senior centurion, was a conspirator, Metellus wouldn't believe it. But a god wouldn't lie.

Superloo heard the clink as Sextus grabbed his trident. 'No weapons,' it warned. 'We mustn't arouse suspicion. They plan to kill all who oppose them, including Metellus.'

'Let them try,' growled Sextus. But he put down the trident. He was already clumping towards the tunnel, his set of tweezers, ear scoop and mirror hanging in a loop on his belt. He checked his hairstyle in the mirror, stiffened a few spikes. Even in an emergency, he had to look good, in case there were ladies about.

'He'll be your guide and bodyguard,' Superloo told Finn. 'And if you come across either of those latrines . . .'

'Don't you dare!' said Finn. 'I've got enough to think about.'

'Look after my servant,' Superloo told Sextus. 'Don't let any harm come to him.'

'What did you say to him?' asked Finn.

'I told him to look after you,' said Superloo.

Finn was touched. That Superloo was so hard to figure out. Just when you thought it only cared about its toilet relatives, it went and surprised you.

'He will be safe with me, Divinity,' Sextus answered the toilet.

Finn went hurrying after Sextus. On his way past, he stuck his hand through the bars and shook the Keeper's hand. 'Don't you worry, Fug, mate. We'll find that key, get you and Briana out of there.'

He didn't make any promises to the bear as he passed its cell. But he hadn't forgotten.

Somehow, he'd find a way to set it free.

'Be careful, Finn,' whispered Superloo as Finn's footsteps faded.

Superloo dimmed its cubicle lights and started to play its favourite song softly, 'Drip, drip, drop little April showers'. A low droning noise also came from the ceiling. Was it humming along?

The Keeper needed some comfort too. He clutched his mother's faded picture as he gazed after Finn. Who was that mysterious boy in the too-big *Birrus Britannicus* who talked a strange language and was the servant of a water god? Who, for some reason, called him *Fug*?

Whoever he was, he was on their side – he was going to get the key that would free them.

'Take care, my friend,' said the Keeper softly. 'There are lots of enemies out there.'

On an impulse he called out the servant's name: 'Finn!'

Finn dashed back. 'What?'

The Keeper took his precious picture from round his neck, the only link with who he really was. 'Here,' he told Finn. 'Wear it, for luck.' He thrust it through the bars.

This time, Finn didn't need a translator. He guessed this was some kind of lucky charm.

'Thanks,' he said, putting the leather thong round his neck.

Then he was off, rushing after the gladiator down the dark tunnel.

In his grand house, next to the Headquarters building, servants were helping Metellus strap on his body armour. But, as they bustled around him, he hardly noticed their presence. He was wondering about his only son, Flaccus. The Fort Commander been thinking about him a lot lately. Flaccus was fourteen now; it was time for his manhood ceremony, when Roman boys got their first shave and first toga.

Metellus thought, *I've been a neglectful father*.

He'd meant to send for Flaccus long before now. But there'd always been one more posting, one more battle to fight for the Empire. He couldn't even remember what the boy looked like – only that, when he was born, he'd had rather large ears. That was the reason for the baby-name he'd been given – *Flaccus*. It meant, *he who has sticky-out ears*.

Now Scrofina said Flaccus was on his way. But she'd been very vague about it.

I must ask her for more details when I get back tonight, he thought.

A servant stood on a stool to put on his red-crested helmet. Metellus buckled the strap.

I'll be glad when tomorrow's golden latrine presentation is over, he thought. Royalty coming upset the fort's routine.

He tried to focus his mind on today. His men depended on him for leadership. It was always dangerous, out on patrol beyond the Wall. But in the last twenty-four hours he'd had reports of revolting natives.

He wasn't too worried though. Anyone who went up against the Roman army, that well-trained war machine, was bound to lose. Especially a rabble who painted themselves blue. And who thought it was a brilliant idea to fight in the nude.

'Stupid,' sighed Metellus, picking up his sword. He felt almost sorry for them.

Pity that Clavus wouldn't be on this patrol. The Senior Centurion was in the fort hospital with some kind of eye disease. That was a big surprise. Metellus had never known Clavus ill – he was as hard as nails.

Two of his other officers had caught the eye sickness; they were in the fort hospital too.

Unluckily, they were the very centurions who'd clubbed together to have the golden latrine made.

Hope they're fit for tomorrow, thought Metellus. It would be a shame if they couldn't be present at the ceremony.

Metellus strapped on his sword. He was without three of his most senior officers. But his men were disciplined. And, besides, they had the lucky latrine standard.

'As long as we have that,' Metellus assured himself, 'the cohort can never be beaten.'

CHAPTER SEVEN

Mr Lew Brush put on his innocent look. It didn't unsettle him, being surrounded by guys with machine guns in camouflage gear. He'd been in trickier situations during the war and managed to bluff his way out of them.

'I'm just bird-watching,' quavered Mr Brush, holding up his toilet-spotting binoculars to show them. 'I'm not doing anything wrong, am I?'

A tall young soldier, the one with the shiniest boots, stepped forward. He looked about twelve years old to Mr Brush. But he was obviously the leader of this special toilet-seeking squad.

'Don't be alarmed, sir,' said the young lieutenant in an American accent. He was friendly – Mr Brush was no threat; he was just a scared and harmless old man.

Mr Brush's wily old eyes glittered briefly. So,

this Special Force had come all the way from America. He should have expected it. The four-billion-dollar microchip that had been put into Superloo by mistake had been meant for a highly secret project at the American Space Travel Research Institute.

'Er, excuse me, sir,' said the lieutenant, lowering his machine gun. 'You don't happen to know if there's a public convenience around here? We're talking the hi-tech kind? Self-cleaning, no-touch flushing, with automatic handwashing facilities?'

Mr Brush gazed vaguely about him, at the rubble-strewn wilderness. 'Round here?' he echoed. 'There's nothing like that round here. And I wish there was – it sounds like luxury. With my weak bladder, I have to go behind a bush.'

'Thanks for your help, sir,' said the polite young lieutenant.

Mr Brush thought they'd move on. He was just thinking, *That was easy*, when one of the soldiers saw the corrugated-iron sheet that Mr Brush had used to conceal Superloo's underground den.

'What's under here, Lieutenant?' he wondered, poking it with his machine gun. 'Didn't they say this rogue toilet was retractable?'

Alarm bells were ringing madly in Mr Brush's head. They were better briefed, more competent, than he thought. They were a crack squad of toilet-hunters, highly trained, their orders coming from the very highest level. Maybe even from the American president himself.

Other soldiers were moving in. 'Careful,' said Mr Brush. 'There's a nest of snakes under there.'

'Snakes don't bother us none, sir,' said one of the special squad. 'We just shoot their heads right off.'

'Errr, did you say you were looking for a public loo?' asked Mr Brush, desperately playing for time while his mind searched for a way to distract their attention from the iron sheet.

Suddenly, he had a brainwave.

'Well, you're in luck,' Mr Brush told the soldiers with new confidence. 'I'm just the bloke you need.'

The young officer looked suspicious. How come this guy hadn't said this before?

Blaster was sitting, wheezing and slobbering over the young soldier's boots. Mr Brush introduced him.

'Meet my Bog Hound,' he said.

'Hi, feller,' said one of the soldiers, putting his hand down to pat Blaster's scabby nose.

'Bog Hound?' asked the young lieutenant. 'What kind of dog is that?'

'Well, you've heard of dogs that sniff out drugs and explosives,' said Mr Brush. 'I've trained this one to sniff out public conveniences.'

'Why?' asked the young officer as he searched Blaster's sad, baggy face for any sign of intelligence. The decrepit old pooch didn't look like it could be trained to do anything. It could barely stand up without falling over.

But Mr Brush had his answer ready.

'I rent him out,' he told the lieutenant. 'I make a good living out of him! Imagine a coach party of old folk on a day trip,' said Mr Brush – he was getting into his stride now. 'Well, when they get out of their coach, what's the first thing they want to do?'

The young lieutenant looked mystified.

'Why, go for a wee, of course. But they're in a strange town. Who knows where the nearest loo is? It's an emergency situation. Some of those old ladies are bursting! They've literally got their legs crossed!'

'Could you get to the point, sir?' said the

young officer. This was way more information than he needed.

'Well, that's where my Bog Hound comes in. Don't you, Blaster?' Blaster looked up adoringly at his master, and wagged his tail feebly. 'All you have to say to him is "Seek!" and he's off, sniffing out the nearest public convenience. Perhaps it's just round the corner, or maybe three streets away.'

'So what does your Bog Hound do when he's found it?' asked the young officer.

'He howls,' said Mr Brush, with another flash of inspiration.

'To let the old folks know where he's at?' asked a soldier eagerly.

'You've got it!' said Mr Brush. He knew now he had them hooked. 'It's a long, mournful howl,' added Mr Brush. 'When the long mournful howl of the Bog Hound echoes through the streets, those old folks know that relief is near. All they have to do is follow that sound! He's in great demand,' said Mr Brush. 'I could rent him out on a coach trip every day.'

'And you make a good living?' asked one of the soldiers. 'It's a great idea! I might start up my own Bog Hound business when I get back to the US.'

The soldier believed him. But the young lieutenant was more sceptical.

'Check out my website,' Mr Brush urged him. 'Homeanddry.com. Check out the extras I offer. You know how rescue dogs carry barrels of brandy? My Bog Hound carries a toilet roll round his neck – the soft, quilted, dimpled kind, for the exclusive use of my customers. You know public loos – either there's no toilet roll left, or it's that horrible hard stuff, very unkind to the bum.'

Now the officer seemed convinced – if it was on the web it must be true. And that detail about the dimpled toilet roll clinched it. 'Say, sir,' he asked, 'could we borrow your Bog Hound?'

Mr Brush thought they'd never ask. He was desperate to get them away from here. Superloo might be coming back to its home base at any moment. 'I'd be proud,' said Mr Brush, 'to offer his services free to the American military.'

Now came the difficult part. Mr Brush looked Blaster in the eye. He pointed his arm dramatically. 'Go seek, boy!' he cried in an urgent voice.

Blaster didn't move. He wasn't the brightest of dogs and he was a bit deaf. He knew his master wanted him to do something, but he had no idea what. He was getting upset, and a faint tooting noise came from his leaky rear end.

Mr Brush felt himself sweating. 'Go, boy!' he urged Blaster again in ringing tones. 'Sniff out that toilet!'

At last Blaster got up. He tottered off in the direction of Mr Brush's pointing finger. Soon the long grass swallowed him up. They waited and waited and waited. How far would Blaster get, Mr Brush wondered, before he looked round and realized his dear old master wasn't behind him?

'I feel like shooting me some snakes,' said a soldier, going to lift up the corrugated-iron sheet.

But then Blaster saved the day. From some-where, in the depth of the wilderness, came a terrible sound. It was so hopeless, so despairing, like the cry of a lost, abandoned soul.

'The long, mournful howl of the Bog Hound!' said Mr Brush. 'He's found it!'

'Move it, men!'

Suddenly the young officer's voice was clipped, commanding. The squad levelled their machine guns, went sprinting off through the bushes.

Phew, that was close, thought Mr Brush, wiping his forehead. He was glad to know his old bluffing skills hadn't deserted him.

But he couldn't relax. Superloo was still in great danger. That Bog Hound story wouldn't fool them for long.

He dragged the corrugated-iron sheet out of the way, so the time-travelling toilet could land safely.

Then he shuffled off through the bushes. He was going to Hi-Tech Toilets. He needed to borrow something. He just hoped he could get it here before either Superloo or those soldiers came back.

CHAPTER EIGHT

Finn came out of the tunnel into the cold, bright morning light. For a moment he was dazzled after the dark. Then he saw where they were.

'We're in the arena,' he whispered, with a chill of horror, staring around him.

But Sextus didn't seem impressed. He'd fought in the real Colosseum, before roaring crowds.

What have I come to? he was thinking. Fighting in a crummy, makeshift arena, in a place no one in Rome had ever heard of, on the very edge of the Empire? His career was really on the skids.

Then he felt ashamed for fretting about his own problems. How could he, when his Emperor's life was in danger? He must find Metellus and take him back to that water god.

Once the Fort Commander knew about the plot, he'd have the conspirators arrested right away. By all accounts he was an honest man, a soldier to his fingertips, who lived only for Rome and duty.

Sextus did wonder why the water god didn't just zap the plotters with a thunderbolt. It would save everyone a lot of trouble. But no doubt the divinity had his reasons. Like he had reasons for wanting those two prisoners freed.

'We must hurry!' said the gladiator.

But Finn was still gazing around him, at the tiers of seats. They were eerily empty now. But soon they'd be packed with howling people. He felt sick; he was shivering, as if an angel of death had wrapped its cold dark wings round him.

They hurried out of the amphitheatre.

'Wow,' breathed Finn, impressed. It was a breathtaking view, over the fort's north ramparts. 'It's like we're on top of the world.'

Hadrian's Wall slithered over the crags like a great, white serpent. Beyond it, dark forests seemed to float in an ocean of mist.

But this was no time to gawp at the scenery. Finn scurried after the gladiator towards the fort's main buildings.

Roman forts were busy places. It was only just after dawn, but already the streets were alive and bustling. Finn was relieved to see he fitted in quite well. Most people seemed to be wearing hooded garments of one sort or another, fastened with big brooches.

Superloo had been right about that, too. You had to hand it to that toilet. When it came to history, it certainly knew its stuff.

A flock of hissing geese flowed round Finn's feet. Troopers sat outside the barracks, cleaning their armour and packing their kitbags. Soon they'd all assemble on the parade ground for roll-call, then march out with Metellus into the wilderness beyond the Wall.

Finn stayed right on the gladiator's heels, as they slid between ox carts and dodged steaming piles of horse dung. Buried deep in his hood, Finn caught glimpses of people – a white-haired old man in a grey cloak, melting into the shadows. A man in a toga, weeping buckets, sad chickens clucking round him.

'What's his problem?' wondered Finn.

Whoops! He'd almost crashed into the gladiator. Sextus had stopped to say 'Hi!' to some lady fans and scratch his mark on the water pots they were carrying.

But now some girls were rushing towards Finn. *Do they think I'm a gladiator too?* thought Finn, alarmed but flattered. Did they want his autograph on their pots?

But no, it seemed to be his toggles that attracted them.

What's this all about? thought Finn. He shrank deeper inside his hood as they tried out the toggles, undoing them, doing them up, exclaiming out loud in surprise and delight. 'Hey, geroff me,' cried Finn, in a panic. 'Haven't you ever seen toggles before?'

A great hand plucked him out of the squealing mob.

'*Phew*,' Finn gasped to Sextus. 'Thanks for that!'

Pausing only to fix his hair, that had been mussed by his lady fans, Sextus was off again, with Finn scurrying behind.

Sextus ducked through a little door in a wall. And suddenly they'd left the crowds behind. They were in a peaceful courtyard, with statues and flowers and a softly burbling fountain. Was this the Fort Commander's house?

'Shhh!' said the gladiator, clumping off in his big, metal-studded sandals.

Finn followed Sextus through another door.

Instantly, the heat hit him. They were in the kitchen. It was chaos! Clay ovens were burning red-hot, while slaves were turning spits or rushing about with wine jars and baskets of food for that afternoon's banquet. Everyone was far too busy to notice them, too scared of Scrofina to glance up even for a second.

The gladiator paused to check his reflection in a copper cooking pot. He tutted, fussily. His hair had wilted in the heat. He stopped to spike it up again.

What's that noise? thought Finn, as he waited.

There it was again: a scrabbling in a clay pot on a wooden bench. There was something alive in there! He lifted the lid, had a look.

He saw six furry tennis balls, lying on top of a pile of walnuts. One tennis ball opened an eye and looked at Finn. Finn saw it had tiny pink paws and whiskers.

Dormice? thought Finn, puzzled. What were they doing here? But they looked well fed. Over-fed, in fact. Their bellies were tight as tiny balloons. He shrugged, put the lid back on and left them.

But the gladiator had seen him looking. '*Mmmm*,' he said, making smacking sounds with his lips.

Wait a minute! thought Finn. There was something he was struggling to remember. Something about Romans and dormice. He'd almost got it. But no, it slipped from his mind again.

Sextus was flexing his pecs at an ancient crone. She had her hands in a pile of rotting fish guts, making the whiffy fish sauce the Romans liked so much. 'Hi, gorgeous,' winked Sextus.

Finn thought, *For heaven's sake! Doesn't he ever stop chatting up ladies?* Finn didn't know that, for a gladiator, one more lady fan might mean the difference between life and death.

'Let's go,' Finn urged his muscly minder. Why were they wasting time hanging around here? They had to find Scrofina and Metellus.

As they were leaving the kitchen, the thing he'd been trying to remember came crashing back into Finn's mind: *The Romans ate stuffed, roasted dormice at banquets! They kept them in special dormouse-fattening pots and fed them on walnuts!*

As Sextus looked on, bewildered, Finn dashed back to the clay pot. He'd got a whole list of people and creatures to save, he didn't need any more. But he just couldn't leave those cute little fatties behind to meet that terrible fate. He'd never forgive himself.

He scooped all six of them out of the pot into his duffel-coat pockets. They snoozed on, whiskers and tiny pink noses twitching, not even noticing they'd been moved.

'Yum, yum,' said Sextus, who thought Finn was nicking them for a snack to eat later.

They crept further into the house. Now they were in the family's posh living quarters, with silk-draped couches and underfloor heating. Finn was sweltering in his duffel coat. But he wouldn't take it off. He felt safer inside it. He just undid the top toggle.

He heard a clanking in the distance. Someone came striding out of another room. He was ready for battle, in full armour, with a sweeping red cloak. *That must be Metellus,* thought Finn.

Metellus yelled out something. Finn guessed it was, 'Who on earth are you?' The Commander drew his sword.

But Finn stood his ground. He didn't feel scared. Sextus would explain what they were doing here. But Sextus was being awfully quiet. Finn couldn't even smell his geranium scent. 'Sextus? Sextus?' hissed Finn. He turned around. The gladiator was nowhere to be seen!

Then he felt a sword point pricking his

throat. Metellus was yelling at him, demanding answers. Finn fell to his knees in terror, and his hood slipped down.

Metellus stopped shouting. A look of amazed disbelief crossed his face. He reached out. Finn cringed, but Metellus was only lifting up the picture around his neck, the one Fug had given him. The Fort Commander stared at it for ages. Then, gently, he moved aside Finn's shaggy hair, inspected his ears.

What's he doing? thought Finn, trembling.

Metellus sheathed his sword. His stern face twisted, just a little, with emotion. 'Flaccus,' he said. He wanted to give the boy a big bear hug. But he wasn't used to showing his feelings. So he just clasped Finn's wrist in a formal greeting. 'Flaccus,' he said. '*Salve.*'

'I'm not Flaccus,' Finn tried to protest. 'I'm Finn.'

But Metellus was convinced. That picture of his long-dead wife and the boy's flappy ears were all the proof he needed. 'Flaccus, my son,' he said again. 'Welcome home.' Even though he couldn't show it, Metellus was delighted at his son's arrival. 'I'm going to make it up to him,' he vowed, 'for being such a bad father.'

He saw now that Scrofina had been lying to him all these years. The poor boy hadn't been properly brought up at all. He couldn't even speak Latin! Just some barbarous language Metellus couldn't understand.

'Never mind,' Metellus told him. 'We'll soon teach you to be a Roman. We'll start right away, with your manhood ceremony. Slaves, find the barber, tell him to bring his sharpest razor. And fetch my son a toga!'

The gladiator was quaking in his sandals. He'd faced lions, tigers and top fighters at the Colosseum. But nothing as scary as this.

He'd been striding along with the water god's servant, when suddenly an arm had reached out and dragged him into a bedroom.

Now Scrofina had him cornered. She'd captured a big star from Rome and she wasn't going to let him escape in a hurry.

She thrust her ferrety face, caked with bear's grease, into his.

'I've always wanted to meet a real, live gladiator,' she purred, batting her eyelids, and puckering up her blood-red lips.

CHAPTER NINE

Metellus shook his head sadly. His only son was little better than a savage. He'd screamed with terror at his first shave. He didn't have a clue how to put on a toga. And he wouldn't be parted from that smelly *Birrus Britannicus*, a thing only the natives wore – he'd had a tug of war with the servants when they'd tried to take it away and burn it. But Metellus didn't blame his son.

I blame myself, thought Metellus. *It's all my fault.* He was determined to teach his son Roman ways.

'We'll take a quick tour of the fort,' he told Finn, hustling him out of the house. 'There's just time, before I go out on patrol.'

Finn thought, *What's going on?*

He'd already been through a nightmare. Some guy had come at him with a big razor, tried to slit his throat. Then he'd got tangled up in a white triangular sheet. He'd almost suffocated! Then they'd tried to steal his duffel coat with his dormice in the pocket. And everyone kept calling him Flaccus and smiling, smiling, like they weren't trying to rob and kill him.

Now he was being dragged round the fort by Metellus. And all the time he was worried sick about the Keeper and Briana, locked in that dark cell. And the gladiator. Where had he got to? Probably fixing his hair somewhere and chatting up the ladies.

He needed to get away from Metellus NOW, run back to Superloo at the amphitheatre, tell it, 'We need another plan.' But Metellus hardly took his eyes off Finn; never let him stray from his side. And Finn couldn't warn the Fort Commander about the plot to kill Hadrian or even say, 'This water god wants to see you.'

I wish I'd learned Latin at school, thought Finn. Now that would have been something really useful.

Metellus was giving a cheery, '*Salvete!*' to some guys squatting in a row on a stone bench. What were they doing?

For heaven's sake! thought Finn, as it dawned on him. They were in the latrines, a public loo with a view on the windy south ramparts. They were all soldiers, apart from one old guy wrapped in a grey cloak, with masses of white hair. Finn thought, 'Haven't I seen him before?'

'Flaccus!' said Metellus, presenting his son to his men. The soldiers shouted out greetings. They were amazed to see Metellus so friendly. He was a good commander, a man you could trust with your life, but not usually the matiest of blokes.

Finn thought, *Am I the only one who finds this embarrassing? Being introduced to people when they're on the loo?*

Then he saw the bum-wiping sponges, in a stone jar. Mr Lew Brush had wanted one of those for his Toilet Museum. He'd be chuffed to bits with it. All Finn had to do was pay a visit to the latrine, pretend to need a bum-wiping sponge, then slip it casually into his pocket.

'No!' Finn shuddered. 'No way am I doing that.' Not even for the guy who'd lent him this brilliant coat. Besides he already had pockets full of dormice. Without thinking, his hand felt around to see if they were still asleep.

Whoops! thought Finn. He'd accidentally scooped one out. The fat tennis-ball body went bouncing down the grassy slope, over the low wall into the latrines. It came to rest by the drainage channel and the jar of bum-wiping sponges. It didn't seem to be hurt – it had as many layers of fat as a baby seal.

But then Finn gasped in horror.

A soldier, still chatting with his mate, reached out towards the sponges, missed, and found something else nice and soft and furry . . .

'No!' howled Finn. He flung himself desperately down into the latrines, past the row of seated soldiers, '*Excuse me!*' and grabbed his dormouse in the nick of time, just as the guy's fingers were closing round it. As Finn stuffed it back in his pocket, he noticed its eyes were still tight shut.

'*Phew!*' sighed Finn. It would never know how close it came to being used as a bum-wiping sponge.

Finn climbed back up the grassy slope towards Metellus, who was shaking his head, a puzzled frown on his face. He couldn't understand this son of his. Why had he dived into the latrines and apparently seized a bum-wiping sponge? If he wanted his own personal one, he only had to ask.

Poor, deprived boy, thought Metellus. He felt

even more guilty. His son seemed to have no belongings, apart from that smelly *Birrus Britannicus*. Even his own bum-wiping sponge seemed like luxury to him.

He wanted to reassure his son, say, 'We'll soon get to know each other. I'll make it up to you for all you've suffered.' But he didn't know how to unbend. All he could think of was to clasp Finn's wrist again in that cold, formal grip.

They were passing the hospital now, where Clavus and the other centurions were recovering from eye sickness. Metellus would have liked to pop in, see how they were doing. But he didn't have time. It was past dawn, the pink had already faded from the sky. Soon the cohort would be on the march. As they crossed the parade ground, Metellus pointed out two young recruits, training with wooden swords. But his son didn't seem impressed. He barely gave them a glance.

But that's because Finn was thinking, *Where's he taking me now?* They were entering another building. 'I don't believe this,' Finn panicked. He recognized this place from pictures in school history books. 'It's a bathhouse.'

They were in the changing room, with alcoves in the wall for your clothes. Guys were undressing, right in front of him, all shapes and sizes. Didn't *anything* make these Romans blush?

We've just got time to strip off, thought Metellus. *Five minutes in the steam room, a plunge in the cold pool, then a quick scrape down with a strigil.*

He tried to help his son out of his *Birrus Britannicus*, show him what you had to do. Bathhouses could be very confusing if you didn't know the routine.

Finn pushed Metellus away, clutched his coat to him. This time it wasn't just his dormice he was worried about. 'I am NOT gonna take my clothes off. NO WAY.'

As Finn fought to keep his duffel coat on, he felt a strange sensation inside it. A creeping, crawling, scrabbling feeling. *There, no, there.* It was all over his body.

This can't be happening, thought Finn. But it was. Some dormice had woken up and chewed their way through a pocket. And now they were exploring beneath his duffel coat. He could see moving bulges as they scampered about.

Metellus was even more confused by his son's weird behaviour. Why didn't he want to undress? Was he ashamed of his body?

But no, thought Metellus. *That couldn't be.* He could plainly see the boy's chest muscles rippling under his coat. He must be very fit. Those pecs on his spear-throwing arm seemed to be swelling as you watched!

Then Metellus had a brainwave. Had he got it all wrong? Totally misunderstood his son? His taking the bum-wiping sponge, his scorn at the wooden swords, his refusal to undress, it all made perfect sense now.

He thinks our Roman ways are soft, decided Metellus. *He's expressing his disapproval.* It was tough in Tungria; men shunned things like baths. And only cissies wiped their bums with sponges. Real men probably used tree bark or jagged flints.

'I understand what you're telling me, my son!' cried Metellus. 'And I admire you for it. Enough of these soft Roman ways, this prancing about with pretend swords! You're saying, "Let's see this army in action!"'

As Metellus clapped his son on the shoulder, a little squeak came from under his *Birrus Britannicus.* Metellus didn't notice; he was too busy apologizing. 'Sorry, Flaccus, my son, I didn't understand. How could I have been so stupid? Come out on patrol with me and my soldiers. I think I can promise you some real fighting!'

*

Sextus staggered out of Scrofina's bedroom. 'What a terrible woman!' he gasped. It was like being attacked by an octopus – her sucker lips all over his face, her tentacle arms squeezing the breath from his body.

He'd forgotten to ask for the key. But no way was he going back in there. What else had the water god commanded? *Find Metellus. Bring him to me!* But the gladiator could hear horns in the distance. He rushed to the fort ramparts. Metellus and the cohort were well beyond the Wall, marching off towards the wilderness, with their lucky latrine standard held proudly aloft.

The fort was almost empty of soldiers, apart from Clavus and the other conspirators. And Hadrian could be arriving at any minute. Plus, the water god's servant was nowhere to be seen. And Sextus had promised the god he'd look after him.

It was all a complete shambles. He'd let the water god down, not to mention his Emperor. He must get back to the amphitheatre right away and confess his failure.

'But the divinity will know what to do,' Sextus reassured himself. Divinities always did.

CHAPTER TEN

Finn was staggering under the weight of his kit. He had no idea Roman soldiers had to lug so much gear about. A cooking pot, tools for camp-building, bags of beans and onions: they were just some of the things he had tied to the fork-shaped stick that was hoisted on his shoulder. And that was besides the shield and javelins and helmet he was carrying. And the dormice asleep in his pocket.

If he had to fight, he'd be a dead man. It would take him half an hour to unload all this stuff before he could face the enemy.

Oh no, it's raining, he thought, peeping out from beneath his duffel-coat hood.

What was that, over there, by that rock? He saw movement, a flash of flaming red.

Finn stared. But where he thought he'd seen something, there was nothing now.

The cohort tramped on into the drizzle.

From somewhere in the wilderness, a wolf howled. Finn shuddered: he felt the hairs creeping on the back of his neck. Even the other soldiers looked nervous. Then an owl hooted, a bad omen.

Someone started a marching song, to keep up their spirits.

Beyond the Wall was a scary place. Those dark forbidding firs seemed to be moving closer. Yellow mist from the bogs writhed like sea snakes around their ankles.

Metellus was on a fine white horse, riding at the front of the column. But he'd thought, *Better put Flaccus in the ranks.* He didn't want the men to think his son was getting special treatment. Besides, Flaccus had already shown he hated soft living. He'd much prefer to rough it with common soldiers.

Finn stumbled on, bent under his load. The lucky latrine standard bobbed at the head of the column, battered but proud, hung with wreaths from its many glorious victories. At the moment, though, rescuing ancient toilets wasn't Finn's top priority. Not when the Keeper, Briana and the bear were in deadly peril. They were all due to die in just a few hours.

You need to get back to the fort, Finn thought frantically. *Just run,* he urged himself.

But it wasn't that easy. He was surrounded by armed soldiers. Would they think he was deserting? Chase him, even chuck spears? And there was another big worry. They were getting further and further away from the Wall, going deeper into the wilderness. Could he ever find his way back on his own?

The soldier marching next to him was limping. He rummaged in his backpack, got out a red stick of something. 'Least I remembered my foot ointment this time,' he said, showing it to Finn.

'Thanks, don't mind if I do,' said Finn taking it and absent-mindedly cramming it into his mouth.

'That's my blister stick!' said the soldier.

What's he on about? thought Finn, chewing. *Hey, these Roman candy bars are quite tasty.*

A warning shout came from Metellus. The singing voices quavered, then stopped. Suddenly a spear whizzed through the air, and thudded into someone's shield.

Now the soldiers around Finn were crouching, shields up, javelins ready. *There!* They could see the enemy. *There!* Figures, light-footed as mountain goats, flitted across the crags. A soldier threw a spear but it missed and clanged off the rocks.

Finn gazed fearfully up to where the figures had been. But there was no one there. Nothing but stillness and silence. Even the forest seemed to be holding its breath.

Ghosts, thought Finn with a shiver.

It was that kind of place, eerie and mystical. Were the soldiers spooked too? They were muttering to each other, eyes flickering everywhere. A shout from an officer made them shut up but they were still jittery.

That howl came again, wild and desolate and very close.

The cohort bunched together, with officers shouting orders. High on the crags, Finn caught a glimpse of a tall figure with fiery red hair. Then it melted into the trees.

'They're everywhere!' said one soldier.

'Why don't they face us like men?'

'Because they're not men, they're spirits.' All soldiers knew about the druids, the priests of the painted people. They had the power to conjure up spirits.

But whether they were men or spirits, the lucky latrine standard would protect the cohort.

An officer reminded them of that: 'Courage, men! So long as we have our latrine, nothing can harm us.'

'There!' cried an officer, pointing his sword.

There were dark, running shapes in the mist. But when they got there, there was no sign, not even footprints.

'There!' The cohort clanked off in another direction.

And all the time, they were being lured further away from the Wall, into unknown territory.

They marched out of the trees, and suddenly found themselves on a grassy plain. It was the perfect place for an ambush. And now the crags around them came alive. There were running figures, savage howls, shrieks that chilled your blood. There seemed to be hundreds of them! The cohort was trapped!

'Form *testudo*!' yelled Metellus, leaping off his horse, giving it a slap to send it galloping back to the fort and safety.

Finn was caught up in the rush to obey the order. Cooking pots, kitbags were thrown aside. Panicking, Finn dumped all his gear, even his spears and shield. He found himself in a sweaty scrum of soldiers.

But what looked like chaos wasn't. They were doing something they'd practised loads of times.

'Form *testudo*!' came the order again.

They were boxing themselves in behind walls of shields, making a roof of shields over their heads. Finn just wasn't quick enough. *Where's everyone gone?* he thought. He looked around. He was the only one left out here. Everyone else, including Metellus, was shut up inside the testudo, packed in tight, like sardines in a tin.

'Let me in!' yelled Finn, hammering on the outside of the shields. But no one in there could hear him. They were too busy clattering those shields from the *inside* and yelling, to scare the enemy.

Desperately, he ran round the *testudo*. The shield wall was solid. There was just one tiny gap, up in the roof, where the lucky latrine standard poked through defiantly.

'Owwww, owwww!' There came those blood-curdling howls again. The cohort began shuffling forward, like a giant, armour-plated centipede.

'Hide!' Finn's brain told him. He hurled himself into the bracken, tunnelled in like a fox.

Inside the *testudo*, the soldier whose blister stick Finn had scoffed felt a *thud* on the shield he was holding above his head.

'They're on the roof!'

'Don't break *testudo*!' yelled Metellus, as the shields sagged under the weight of more bodies.

Only Finn, peeping out from his hiding place, saw what was really happening. With wild war whoops, blue-painted warriors came springing down from the crags, their cloaks spread like wings. They landed on the shields and raced lightly across them. *Whump*, someone heavier than the rest landed. It was Birte, the warrior queen, swinging her axe, her magnificent red hair streaming behind her. She pounded across the *testudo*, plucked out the lucky latrine standard on her way and leapt down the other side, still running.

She only had a handful of men with her. They looked like a wild and unorganized bunch. How had they seemed to be so many, in so many places at once? No wonder the Roman soldiers thought they were supernatural.

Finn watched as they raced away, jabbing the standard in the air in triumph. They paused only to turn round for a moment to mock their enemy, still locked up inside the *testudo*.

Gosh, that's cheeky, thought Finn, as Birte made some very rude gestures and two of her warriors turned round, lifted their tunics and waggled their bare, hairy bums.

Birte bellowed, 'I've got your standard and now I'm going to get my daughter!' Then they all vanished into the forest.

Finn saw his chance to get back to Superloo. As the shields unlocked and the *testudo* broke up, he started to run.

Metellus came out from behind his shield. He couldn't believe the disgrace. How would the cohort ever live it down? Their precious standard had been stolen. And, to make things worse, was that his son Flaccus deserting the field of battle? The famous Roman army discipline was in tatters. Without their lucky standard his soldiers had lost their courage. They should have been ruthlessly hunting down the enemy, rescuing their standard. But they were just standing around, talking about spirits and magic in small, scared voices, like frightened children.

'Remember our watchwords, men!' cried

Metellus. 'Strength and Honour! We are Roman soldiers. We're not scared of ghosts, are we?'

'Oh yes we are!' a hundred quavering voices answered.

CHAPTER ELEVEN

'So All-powerful Divinity,' said Sextus. 'What do I do now?'

Superloo sighed. It was getting fed up with being a god. At first it had liked all the adoration. After all, who wouldn't worship a toilet with a brain as big as planet? But now it was sick of being pestered. It felt quite sorry for itself.

'*Problems, problems,*' it murmured in self-pitying tones. It was surrounded by idiots. Couldn't these humans get anything right?

'So you have dared to return without Metellus, *or* the key, *or* my servant?' it thundered in an angry bellow, even though it was bored with the whole god-thing. It just wanted to find its toilet ancestors and get out of here. 'Can't you mortals sort out your own mess?' it demanded.

'Wait a minute,' said the Keeper from inside his cell. 'Me and Briana wouldn't be in this mess if it wasn't for you.'

The gladiator was shocked, 'You can't talk to a divinity like that.'

But Superloo was thinking, 'Didn't Finn say the same thing?' Perhaps it was just a *tiny* bit responsible for their imprisonment. It wondered where Finn was. 'He'll be back,' Superloo assured itself. Finn always came back. Didn't he?

'I don't need him,' Superloo tried to convince itself.

But, suddenly, it felt its computer brain faltering. Was its power already running low? Would it have to go back to the twenty-first century to re-charge? But no, this was something different. Its bouncy self-confidence, its certainty about everything, had suddenly crumbled. It was having the computer equivalent of a panic attack.

'I can't cope,' it moaned. 'I wish Finn would come back. I wish they'd all just GO AWAY AND LEAVE ME ALONE!'

If it had been human, it would have hidden under its duvet. What could a public convenience do to hide from the world? It shut its door tight. Instantly the cells and tunnels were plunged into darkness. It switched on its 'BUSY' sign.

'Divinity? Divinity?' bellowed Sextus. 'Tell us your bidding!'

But no sound came from the shrine. Its door was shut tight. It seemed the divinity had abandoned them.

'You made the water god angry with your rudeness,' Sextus told the Keeper.

'Someone's coming!' Briana interrupted.

They heard the sinister clashing sound of metal on metal. Then a shrill voice cried, 'Girl, where are you?'

It was Scrofina, come with her iron shears to chop off Briana's hair. Her wig maker was going to have to work like the clappers to get it ready for this afternoon's ceremony. Even with Scrofina screeching at him, he might not manage it. But it would be a big waste for hair like that to get all mauled and bloody in the arena.

The Keeper held his breath. Sextus drew back. Hidden in the shadows, he heard the jangling of keys. Did she have the guards with her?

'Curses,' muttered Scrofina. 'I can't see a thing.'

She peered into the cells. The first was empty, and the second. She was getting impatient – Scrofina wasn't used to waiting for what she wanted. She heard a low moan from the third cell. 'Is that you, girl?' she demanded. She saw a dark shape huddled at the back, a white eyeball. She jammed a key into the lock and turned it, yanked the door open. 'You should be honoured, girl. Your hair will be meeting the Emperor today, even if you won't.'

But Scrofina didn't have time to laugh at her own cruel joke: '*Aaaargh!*' Something big and shaggy hurled itself from the back of the cell. She saw slashing claws, snarling fangs. She smelled hot, stinking breath. She dropped the shears and the keys. With another piercing shriek she turned and fled.

The bear lumbered after her, out of the dark tunnels into the bright arena. Did it see her as its first decent meal for days? Or was it her bear's grease make-up that attracted it? Whatever it was, it seemed very keen to catch up with her.

'Help me!' screamed Scrofina, as it chased her out of the amphitheatre and towards the North Gate. Several of her servants were rushing about on errands. But they seemed not to hear her cries – she shouldn't have made their lives such a misery.

She rushed through the North Gate with the bear growling behind. Some sentries on the fort ramparts hurled their spears. But Scrofina should never have had that solider flogged for calling her ferret-face.

'Oh dear, we missed the bear,' said one sentry.

'By miles,' sniggered the other. They watched Scrofina and the bear disappear into the wilderness. The drizzle had stopped. The sun was coming out, burning off the mist. It looked like being a lovely day.

Back at the amphitheatre Sextus was picking up the dropped keys, trying them in the lock of the Keeper and Briana's cell. One fitted.

'We're free!' said Briana, as the door creaked open and they stumbled out.

'And the bear has escaped,' added Sextus. 'That means there will be no entertainment today.' Sextus was glad about that. He hadn't wanted to see the Keeper and Briana die. He hadn't wanted to kill the bear either.

I just want my freedom, he thought. *And maybe, after that, a little farm to settle down on.*

But the dangers weren't over. 'What about my Emperor?' said Sextus. 'Clavus and the others are still planning to kill him. We must do something.' The shrine was as silent as before, the door tight shut. The divinity wasn't communicating. So it was up to them, mere mortals, to help themselves.

'We must get Metellus and the cohort back here fast,' said the gladiator. 'Someone must send a signal.'

The Keeper looked at Briana. The same thought was in both their heads. Why should they care about the Emperor? The sensible thing to do was run, while they had the chance. After all, they were still criminals, under sentence of death.

Then Briana sighed. 'I suppose we can't just let him die,' she said.

'All right,' said the Keeper. 'I'll send the signal.' Since it was his dearest wish to be a soldier, he'd studied everything soldiers do. He'd watched them send signals many times. 'But we'll have to do it from the roof of the Headquarters building.'

'Right,' said Sextus. 'Let's go.'

'You don't have to come,' said the Keeper to Briana. 'You should escape while you can.'

'Not likely,' said Briana, who'd inherited her mother's fiery spirit as well as her flaming red hair. 'Have you got a spare sword?' she asked the gladiator.

'No weapons,' warned Sextus. The few sentries Metellus had left would arrest them immediately. 'And you two, don't let the sentries see you. You're supposed to be still locked up.'

'But what about the conspirators? What if we meet them?'

'Don't worry. They'll stay out of sight in the hospital until Hadrian shows up.'

And that wouldn't be long now. It must be noon already.

'Even if we do send a signal,' fretted Sextus, 'can Metellus get back in time?'

'I don't know,' said the Keeper. 'But we've got to try.'

Pausing only to pluck out a chest hair, '*Ouch!*', the gladiator led the way. His sandals *slap-slapped* ahead, while gusts of geranium-scented oil wafted behind him. From the closed shrine, in its dark corner, came a low droning sound. It was the divinity, playing, 'Drip, drip, drop little April showers', and humming along.

*

In the forest, Finn was lost. He was desperate to get back to the fort and Superloo but all these trees looked the same. He turned round dizzily. Which way should he go now? Had he been walking in circles?

He heard a crashing in the bracken. Quickly, he hid himself. Scrofina came stumbling out of the trees. She looked a wreck – but she couldn't stop to repair her make-up. That frightful creature wasn't far behind. It was a good job it was weak from lack of food, or it would have caught her by now. She plunged back into the trees. Then a bear came shambling through. It stopped to claw some berries from a bush and grind them up in its jaws.

Finn's heart leapt with joy. He recognized that mangy coat, those yellow, snaggly teeth, those soulful eyes.

It escaped! he thought. And another thing occurred to him too. All he had to do, to find the fort, was go in the direction they'd come from.

As soon as the bear had gone, he left his hiding place and set off. It was an easy trail to follow – the bear's heavy body had broken branches, and scraps of Scrofina's fine silk robes fluttered from thorn bushes.

The Wall! thought Finn. He could see it, gleaming and whitewashed in the distance, cresting the craggy hills like a roller-coaster. He broke into a run.

When Sextus, Briana and the Keeper reached the roof of the Headquarters building, the signal brazier was already smouldering.

'Someone's been using it,' said the Keeper. What for? And who were they signalling to?

Briana thought she'd seen the white-haired old man, wrapped in his grey cloak, slip down as they came up. But she couldn't be sure. That old man gave her the creeps, prowling around, listening and lurking in dark corners.

But she couldn't worry about him now. She and the gladiator stood on watch, while the Keeper fanned the tiny flame. A basket of fresh grass was kept by the brazier. He fed some in to make it smoke. Soon a dark column rose high into the blue sky.

Out in the forest, beyond the Wall, Metellus saw the thin black trickle of smoke.

'The fort's under attack!' he cried. Time to rally his men. 'Are you going to let those painted savages defeat you, take your lucky latrine standard?' he roared. 'You should be ashamed to call yourselves Roman soldiers! On your feet! Seize your weapons! We're not going to march. We're going to *run!*'

But someone else saw the smoke too. Clavus and the other conspirators were in the fort hospital, waiting for the Emperor's arrival.

'Not long now,' said Clavus. 'He'll be here within the hour.'

Like a caged tiger, he paced up and down the ward, and stared out of the window. Suddenly he frowned. 'Someone's signalling from the Headquarters roof!' He snatched up his sword. 'You stay here,' he told the others. 'I'll deal with this.'

CHAPTER TWELVE

Finn took down his duffel-coat hood. He'd slipped into the North Gate in the confusion when some squealing piglets escaped from a cart. He'd dodged a lady admiring his toggles. And now he was back under the amphitheatre.

He had to grope his way along. Why was it so dark? Where was Superloo's cubicle light? He stumbled past the bear's open cell.

'Fug? Briana?' he called, his voice echoing in the tunnels. But their cell was empty too. And there was no sign of Sextus anywhere. The whole place seemed deserted.

Finn felt a sick chill round his heart. Had Superloo abandoned him in the second-century AD with nothing but a duffel coat and six overfed dormice?

'Please, please, let it be here,' he whispered, as he crept on into the gloom.

Then he felt a great giddy *whoosh* of relief. He could see a 'BUSY' sign flashing in the shadows.

Good old faithful Superloo! He should have known it wouldn't leave without him. Finn went rushing up. It was a bit battered and dented but he could have thrown his arms around it, given the public convenience a big cuddle. He beat on the closed door.

'Open up, Superloo,' he cried. 'I'm back! Where is everyone? What's been going on?'

But the door stayed firmly shut. Finn hammered on it some more. 'It's me!'

No answer.

'Are you sulking?' he asked finally. Still no response. 'I've got loads to tell you,' coaxed Finn.

Slowly, Superloo's door slid open. Finn stepped into its silver inside. The cubicle lights were softly glowing.

'Is that you, Finn?' asked a tremulous little voice from the ceiling. 'I'm so glad you're back.'

Finn felt a warm glow all over. The super-intelligent loo really seemed to have missed him. 'What's the matter?' he asked it. 'Were you worried about me?'

He went gabbling on, telling the toilet how he'd been mistaken for someone called Flaccus, been forced to go on patrol, and everything else that had happened since.

'Wait a minute,' Superloo interrupted him. Its voice seemed suddenly strong and confident, back to its usual know-all self. 'You mean, you were *this* close to the lucky latrine and you didn't nick it?'

'You must be joking,' said Finn. 'This fierce warrior woman got there before me.'

'Did she have a roar like an angry bull?' asked Superloo.

'Yes,' shuddered Finn. 'And red hair. And muscles like the Incredible Hulk.'

'That's Briana's mum,' said Superloo. 'Queen Birte. She's that frightful woman who attacked me.'

Its voice changed again. It began to snivel. Finn felt like handing it a piece of bog roll, saying, 'Here, wipe your nose.' But, of course, he kept forgetting, Superloo wasn't human.

'My poor latrine relative,' it sobbed. 'How am I going to get it back? And I haven't even got the golden replica.'

Finn felt himself going mushy inside; he just couldn't help it. He knew how much its toilet relatives meant to Superloo. And there was another thing. The toilet genius didn't like failing. It wouldn't go back to the twenty-first century without at least *one* historically important toilet.

'Look, if I get the golden replica for you,' said Finn, '*then* can we go back home?'

'Absolutely!' boomed Superloo, making a miraculous recovery from its crying fit.

'But what about the others?' asked Finn. 'Briana and the Keeper and Sextus. Are they OK?'

'Yes, you needn't worry about them,' said Superloo breezily. 'They're busy foiling the assassination plot. You just concentrate on getting me the golden latrine.'

'Where is it?' asked Finn, who was already regretting his rash promise.

'In the Temple of Mithras. Just past the bathhouse. It should be easy peasy. Just *nip* in and take it and *nip* out. There'll be nobody there.'

'Then we'll go?' asked Finn. 'Even if you *haven't* got the lucky latrine?' He needed to make doubly sure. He must never forget that the toilet could be very cunning. It would do anything to get what it wanted.

'Of course,' answered Superloo in its silkiest tones. 'Sometimes, you just have to compromise.'

'Remind me, though,' said Finn, 'to give *this* back before we go.' He touched the tiny portrait on the leather thong round his neck. 'Metellus was really interested in Fug's lucky charm.'

'His name's not Fug,' quacked Superloo. 'Where'd you get that from?'

'It's written on his forehead!'

'I've been doing some thinking,' said Superloo. 'And I'll tell you what his name really is. It's not Fug, or Keeper. It's Flaccus. He's the *real* Flaccus – *he who has sticky-out ears*. And Metellus is his father.'

'Wow!' said Finn. 'Cool! You sure about this?'

'I am never wrong,' said Superloo. 'Besides, it's a fairly simple conclusion. Even your poor human brain should have worked that out.'

'Wait a minute,' said Finn. Something frightful had just occurred to him. 'If Metellus mistook me for his son Flaccus, *he who has sticky-out ears*, does that mean *I* have sticky-out ears?'

'No, no,' said Superloo soothingly. 'Of course you don't.'

'How do you know?' demanded Finn. 'You can't see.'

'Because,' said Superloo, its devious brain whirring, 'I could tell. If your ears were big and flappy, you know like Dumbo's, they'd make a breeze as you move around. And my finely tuned sensors would detect it.'

'My ears aren't like Dumbo's, are they?' roared Finn, aghast. How come nobody had told him before? Were they afraid of hurting his feelings? 'I'm *never* gonna get a girlfriend,' Finn fretted.

'For heaven's sake,' snapped Superloo. 'You humans are so insecure. Stop fussing about your ears, will you? Your ears are perfectly fine. Now go and find my toilet relative!'

Finn frowned, 'Well, if you're certain.'

His ears were one part of his body he'd never had problems with. But now he put up his duffel-coat hood, in case anyone laughed at them.

'Aren't you gone yet?' asked Superloo.

'I'm going, I'm going,' protested Finn. 'Just one more question.'

'It's not about your ears, is it?'

'No, it's about Fug, I mean Keeper, I mean Flaccus, whatever you call him! Anyway, does

he know who he *really* is? Does he know that
he's Metellus's son?'

'No,' said Superloo. 'I'm absolutely certain
he doesn't.'

Up on the roof of the Headquarters building,
the Keeper said, 'I've run out of fresh grass.'

He just hoped Metellus had seen their call
for help – there was still a trail of black smoke
hanging in the sky.

Briana looked down from the roof. The fort
was strangely empty of soldiers. But it was still
busy, with servants, traders, ox carts, animals.
Then she saw a red centurion's crest pushing
through the crowd, a hawk face beneath the
helmet.

She turned, horrified, to the others. 'It's
Clavus, he's armed. He's coming this way.'

'He's seen the smoke,' said Sextus. They'd
all known it was a risk.

Clavus fixed his eyes on the roof. '*Ha!*' he
said to himself. He could see blond hair spikes.
It's that pretty-boy gladiator, he thought, his lip
curling. *I knew there was something fishy about him.*

Clavus clanked through the Headquarters
building. When he got up to the roof, there
was nothing there, except for a smoking

brazier and a faint whiff of geraniums. Sextus had slipped away, down the steps that led into the alley.

But Clavus knew where to find him. He already had his sword but he grabbed a spear on his way out, from one of the guards. He was the finest swordsman in the cohort, ruthless in battle. His middle name was 'No Mercy'.

He gave a grim smile. It would be almost too easy. That preening peacock would be up against a real professional. Gladiators couldn't really fight; it was all show, for the crowds. And anyway, this one was only a slave with a nicked ear, not worth a fig. He'd soon have Sextus on his knees, begging for his life.

But I'm afraid, thought Clavus, *that, this time, it's* definitely *going to be thumbs down.*

CHAPTER THIRTEEN

'Is that you, Divinity?' called Briana. A dazzling beam came from the shrine again, flooding the tunnels and cells with light.

'Yes!' boomed Superloo. 'It is I, the all-powerful water god!'

It was in high spirits, now Finn had gone off to fetch the golden latrine. And, secretly, it hadn't totally given up hope of getting the lucky latrine standard as well. It felt back in control again, full of confidence. But the humans seemed a bit worked up about something.

'Clavus is outside in the arena,' explained the Keeper. 'He's calling for Sextus to come and fight him.'

'So?' snapped Superloo. It hadn't got time for petty human problems. It was too busy thinking about its toilet ancestors.

Of course, they're only poor, primitive creatures compared to ME, mused Superloo. *At a basic stage of toilet evolution, with not a brain cell between them.* But they *were* family after all. And an important part of toilet heritage. With them gathered around it, Superloo wouldn't feel so alone. Although its greatest dream was, one day, to meet a toilet with its own brain power. A toilet you could have intelligent conversations with . . .

'Divinity?' said Briana, breaking into its thoughts. 'Are you listening? Sextus is in his dressing room. He says his hair's a mess. His tunic's dirty. He says he can't go out to fight looking like that.'

'Cha!' replied Superloo scornfully. 'Do you humans need help with every little thing?'

It hated being interrupted when it was daydreaming – didn't these humans realize that public conveniences also had plans, ambitions?

'Just tell Sextus to come here,' it snapped, with a long-suffering sigh.

The gladiator came clumping over. 'So what's your problem?' said the water god, tetchily.

From outside in the arena, Clavus bellowed,

'Are you coming out, gladiator? Or do I have to come in there to get you?'

'Divinity, I can't face my public like this,' fussed the gladiator. 'That dressing room just doesn't have the facilities: no scented oil, no pigeon dung. And I haven't even had time to pluck my underarm hair.'

'For heaven's sake,' said the Keeper. 'Forget about your armpits!'

But the gladiator couldn't help it. If he didn't look his best, he just couldn't fight. And it was more than that. In his heart of hearts, he didn't want to. He was even wondering if he'd lost his skills.

'Step inside my shrine,' said Superloo.

Puzzled, Sextus clumped in. Superloo's door slid shut. The 'CLEANING' sign lit up on its silver wall. From inside came a sound like water gurgling, then *whirring*, like a washing machine starting up. Superloo stated to rock. It was going through a speeded-up version of its cleaning cycle, giving the gladiator a quick wash-down with its water jets. There was a *whooshing* sound, like a giant hair dryer, as it blasted him with warm air, then sprayed him with piney-fresh scent. The door slid open again.

'Wow! said Sextus, staggering slightly. He checked his look in Superloo's mirror.

His tunic had never been so snowy-white. His hair looked different. But, 'I like it!' he decided. It was big hair, puffed out all round his head like a blond cloud. And best of all, he smelled fabulous, like a forest glade. Would the ladies approve?

'You look gorgeous,' said Superloo rather impatiently. 'You could take on a whole army.'

Suddenly the gladiator felt his confidence surging back.

'Let me at him!' he roared, rushing out of the cubicle, grabbing his net and trident. He paused only to cry, 'Thank you, Water God!' Then he was gone.

The Keeper frowned. He wished he felt as confident. But could anyone that vain, that bothered about body hair, really be such a good fighter? Well, they'd soon see. He and Briana hurried after the gladiator, out into the sun-soaked arena, where Clavus was waiting.

'Tell me what's happening!' cried Superloo, unable to follow. It was at moments like this that it was really frustrating being a public convenience. It could travel through time but, once there, it was stuck wherever it landed.

'Sometimes I'd give anything,' sighed Superloo wistfully, 'to have legs.'

Out in the arena, the Keeper's sense of foreboding grew. Clavus looked tough, professional, battle-hardened. His hawk face had a mocking smile as if he thought it was hardly worth getting his sword bloody. While Sextus was fluffing his new hair style the Keeper put a hand up to grasp the lucky charm round his neck. But then he remembered – he'd lent it to the water god's servant.

Suddenly, Clavus sprang into action. His spear, as he chucked it, was just a blur. 'Look out!' cried Briana. She was sure Sextus would be skewered.

But he surprised them both. In one casual move, he dropped his mirror and stepped aside. The spear missed him by centimetres. It stuck, quivering, in the sand.

'Cool,' said Finn, who'd just come panting back with the golden latrine seat hidden under his duffel coat.

The gladiator was used to vast roaring crowds in the Colosseum. Now his audience was tiny: just three people. Plus a mystery watcher no one had noticed yet, high up in the top tier of seats.

Clavus snarled with anger. He had no time for fancy gladiator tricks.

'Come on, slave,' he taunted. 'Let me teach you how soldiers fight.' He grasped his sword and charged.

Suddenly Sextus dropped into a tiger crouch.

That's more like it, thought the Keeper. He should have had faith. Anyone who could survive as long in the Colosseum as Sextus must be more than just a pretty face. He had to be a good fighter too. And this guy was better than good – he was a wizard with that net and trident.

Sextus swirled his net. It caught Clavus's sword arm, but he swapped his sword to his left hand and hacked himself free. Now the two fighters were circling, never taking their eyes off each other. There was dead silence in the arena. The little audience watched, hardly daring to breathe.

Suddenly Sextus stabbed with his trident. Clavus lunged, his sword flashing. But Sextus was somewhere else! He'd darted, quick as a lizard, to snatch up his net. Clavus spun round and charged again. The net licked out like a chameleon's tongue and wrapped around him.

He bellowed with rage, slashing at it. He crashed into the sand, still struggling wildly. But it was useless, the net had him trapped. Sextus came pounding up and stood over him with the trident. He'd won, and a quick check in his mirror told him he'd done it all without ruffling his hair.

Just as he'd done countless times in the Colosseum, he looked up. Would his audience give a thumbs up, or thumbs down? Not one of them made a sign; they were all too stunned by his fighting skills.

Then from the highest tier of seats came a mighty shout. They all looked up. For a moment their eyes were dazzled by a golden sunburst. What was up there? Then the sunburst stuck out its arm. And they could clearly see the turned-up thumb.

'It's the old man!' said the Keeper. He'd opened his cloak to reveal a splendid golden breastplate, embossed and decorated and hung with golden laurel wreaths. Now he threw the cloak off completely and took off his old man's wig.

'Emperor!' cried Sextus, thumping his clenched fist against his chest in salute.

'Gladiator!' Hadrian shouted back. 'I

congratulate you on your victory. But don't kill that conspirator. I want to take him in chains to Rome.'

Hadrian came striding down into the arena. He saw conspiracies everywhere. But this time he'd been right. Since yesterday he'd been hanging around the fort in disguise, listening, watching. He'd been suspicious from the start about that golden latrine presentation. His spies had warned him that Clavus couldn't be trusted.

'I've signalled to my Praetorian Guard,' he said. 'They'll be here within the hour.'

The others fell on their knees before the Emperor's shining presence. But Finn was already sneaking back into the tunnel to give Superloo the gold replica and say, 'I've got it! Now let's go home!'

Out in the arena, Sextus had eyes only for his Emperor. He couldn't believe the words that were coming from Hadrian's mouth.

'In honour of your great victory,' the Emperor was saying, 'I give you your freedom. You are a slave no longer.'

The documents to prove it would come later. But for now, the word of an emperor was more than enough. Overcome, Sextus blurted out his thanks. Then he lifted his bowed head and looked round at his audience. They weren't there. The water god's servant had vanished. And the Keeper and Briana had gone too. Just as the gladiator was going to beg Hadrian to pardon them.

But he couldn't worry about them now. He had to get Clavus, the evil conspirator, to the jail in the Headquarters building.

'Come on, you!'

Sextus hauled Clavus to his feet. He didn't notice that, through the net meshes, Clavus didn't look defeated. He still had that mocking little smile on his face.

CHAPTER FOURTEEN

'You promised!' said Finn furiously. 'I did what you wanted. I got you the golden replica. You *promised* we'd go home.'

'I was only wondering,' wheedled Superloo, 'if there was any chance at all of getting the lucky latrine standard.'

'No! No! No!' cried Finn.

He was thinking, *It's time you put your foot down.* Sometimes you had to be firm with Superloo, for its own good. When it came to rescuing its toilet relatives, it never knew when to quit.

'I *told* you!' Finn said sternly. 'Birte's got it. I don't know where she is. We might *never* find her.'

'But . . .' began the toilet.

'Look on the bright side,' urged Finn. 'At least you've got one toilet relative.'

'But it was the original latrine I *really* wanted,' wailed the toilet.

'Look, I went into that creepy temple to get this one,' said Finn. 'You should be grateful!'

'I am, I am,' said the toilet hastily. 'But I was just wondering . . .'

'No!' Finn interrupted. 'Forget it! Don't even *think* about it! No way am I getting the other one. Take me back to the twenty-first century NOW!!'

Superloo could see that, this time, Finn wasn't going to budge. It gave a big, huffy sigh. 'Well, all right,' it said. 'I suppose I *do* need to re-charge. And one toilet relative per trip is a good result . . .'

'Are we off then?' said Finn, anxious to get going while Superloo was being co-operative.

'We're off,' said Superloo, still sounding sulky.

Finn checked in his pockets. Would the trip back wake up his dormice? But they were snoozing away, full of walnuts, twitching every so often like dogs do in their sleep.

'Where shall I put the replica latrine?' asked Finn. He didn't fancy it flying around the cubicle while they time-travelled.

'Look at this,' said Superloo, who'd suddenly perked up. Like an excited child showing Finn a secret, it slid open a panel in its smooth silver walls and revealed a hidden storage compartment.

'I didn't know you had cupboards,' Finn said.

'There's lots of things you don't know about me,' said Superloo smugly. It didn't let on that it didn't know it had cupboards either, until it accidentally found them. Like a curious baby, there were new things about its body and brain that it was discovering every day.

'Hey, King Tut's toilet is in there,' said Finn. He'd been meaning to ask what had happened to that. 'And my Ancient Egyptian clothes! How'd you get them in there?' he asked Superloo. As far as he remembered, he'd left them on the cubicle floor.

'Easy-peasy,' said Superloo. 'I just slid them in. Or at least my floor did. It's on rollers, for cleaning purposes.'

'Cool!' said Finn.

But Superloo didn't need its movable floor when it had a human to do all its little chores. 'Put the latrine inside,' it instructed Finn. Then it slid the cupboard door shut.

'I'm ready,' said Finn, taking a deep breath and hugging the toilet bowl.

The digital clock numbers were whirring, the lights flashing off and on.

'Blast off!' shrieked Superloo.

Then the cubicle started spinning and Finn's world was a silver blur.

He felt the usual dragging wind, almost wrenching his arms out of their sockets. Then something slapped into his eye.

It was the lucky charm that Flaccus had given him, flying out round his neck. 'Stop!' yelled Finn.

Superloo seemed to slam on the brakes. It stopped dead, as if hovering in time. 'What now?' it said tetchily.

'We've got to go back. I've still got Fug's charm.'

'So?' said Superloo.

Dizzily, Finn tried to collect his wits. 'But I've got to give it back. And I've got to tell Fug who he really is.'

'No way,' said Superloo. 'We're almost home. A minute ago, you couldn't wait to get there.'

'Please,' said Finn passionately. 'Please can we go back to the fort? Else Fug could go through his whole life and never know that Metellus is his dad.'

'*Cha!*' said Superloo scornfully, as if Finn was making a big fuss about nothing.

But its computer brain was whirring. And something deep inside its circuits responded. It knew what it felt like, not having a family, feeling that you were alone in the world.

'All right,' it said finally. 'But we can't stay long. My power supplies are running low.'

'Thank you, thank you,' said Finn, amazed that the toilet genius had agreed. But, he should have remembered, Superloo was full of surprises.

They landed with a *whump* back in Roman Britain. Finn staggered to his feet. Superloo's silver door slid open. Finn heard birdsong. He saw sunlight dappling through trees.

'This isn't inside the fort,' he said.

'I think it's the grove where I landed before,' said Superloo. 'I *might* have made a slight miscalculation.'

'It doesn't matter!' cried Finn. 'They're here!'

The Keeper and Briana skidded to a stop. They'd decided to make themselves scarce. Emperors can be very unpredictable. Hadrian might show mercy and pardon them. But he might not. He might order them to be locked up again, even executed. So they'd decided to go on the run beyond the Wall. Perhaps they'd be outlaws forever.

The Keeper, so far as he knew, had no one

to leave behind – except his master the augur and the sacred chickens. But Briana was leaving her family. She wished now that she and her mum had made up. It was only their stubborn pride that had stopped them. Now they might never see each other again.

Briana said: 'Look, Keeper, it's the water god's shrine. How did it get back here?' But she wasn't all that surprised. Divinities can do anything.

And here was the water god's servant – that strange boy in the *Birrus Britannicus*, with those clever fastenings, who spoke some barbaric language. He was waving his arms about, getting very excited. What did he want them to do? Go inside the shrine?

They all crowded in. And now the divinity's voice boomed out.

'Keeper,' the god said, 'I have something to tell you.'

After the god had finished, the Keeper looked dazed.

He hardly noticed when the water god's servant took the charm from round his neck and placed it over his own head.

'Here, Fug, it's yours,' said Finn. 'It's proof of who you are.'

For some reason, Finn couldn't call him Flaccus. That silly baby name just didn't suit him. And anyway, if his ears had stuck out before, they didn't now. But Finn was still worried about his own ears. Were they really too flappy? He'd heard you could have an operation, to pin them back.

The Keeper hadn't stopped looking stunned, disbelieving. *No wonder*, thought Finn. *He's just found out who his dad is.*

'Keeper,' said Briana, who, it seemed, couldn't call him Flaccus either, 'you must stay, make yourself known to Metellus.'

'No,' said the Keeper, shaking himself, as if he'd just woken up from a dream. 'Nothing's changed. We'll go on the run together. Why should Metellus want *me* as a son? They say he's a proud man. And I'm a slave. I've got "FUG" branded on my forehead! He'll just be ashamed of me.'

Briana was going to argue. But then they heard some miserable clucks through Superloo's open door. The Keeper knew that sound.

'Augur!' he cried, rushing outside. It was his old master, surrounded by all his sad chickens, searching the wilderness for the sacred cockerel.

The augur could hardly believe his eyes. He thought he was seeing a ghost. 'Keeper!' he cried. 'It is really you? I thought you were condemned to die!'

He'd been weeping with grief before and made his toga all soggy. But now he was weeping tears of joy.

'Thank goodness you're back,' he sobbed, his tears flowing like a fountain. 'I was lost without you. I just went to pieces. I couldn't predict a thing!'

You couldn't do that anyway, thought the Keeper. But now wasn't the time to point that out. The augur had been a kind master.

The Keeper clapped him on the shoulders. 'Don't cry, I'm here now.' He couldn't tell his master that their reunion would be brief. That, any minute now, he and Briana were leaving.

But then Superloo's sensors felt the ground vibrating. Its hearing system detected jingling armour and its E-nose blister ointment.

'Quick, get inside my shrine,' said Superloo. 'There are soldiers coming.'

The augur crowded in with his sacred chickens. Superloo closed its door. It had never had such a crush in its cubicle.

'It could be the Praetorian Guard,' said the

Keeper. 'Hadrian said he'd sent for them.'

'Or it could be your father, Metellus,' said Briana, 'coming to answer your signal.'

The Keeper stared at her. Those words 'your father, Metellus' made him feel really peculiar. It still hadn't sunk in. And what about Scrofina? Didn't that make her his step-mother? But the Keeper didn't want to think about that. With any luck, she was inside a bear by now.

Suddenly, from outside, they heard a savage war cry. Briana recognized that rebel yell. *Mum!* she thought.

'Open the door!' she commanded. 'I want to see outside.'

Superloo thought, *Cha! That girl's just like her mother*. But it slid open its door. Everyone rushed out. Except for the sacred chickens, who huddled behind the toilet bowl, looking depressed.

Hidden in the grove of trees, the augur, Briana, the Keeper and Finn saw what was happening. There was a wide, scrubby stretch of ground between the grove and the fort. And it was about to become a battlefield.

'There's Mum!' cried Briana. They could see her flaming red hair in the distance.

Around Birte, other painted tribesmen were rising from the heather. 'There's my uncle,' said Briana, pointing to a burly warrior with long dangling moustaches, a double-headed axe, and his arms and chest covered in blue whorls.

Birte, who didn't know her daughter had escaped, had crept up with her warriors right under the fort walls. They'd been about to launch a surprise attack, scale the ramparts with ropes and rescue Briana. But Metellus coming back had ruined their plans. Now, with her tiny band, she turned to face the cohort.

'Surrender!' yelled Metellus. They didn't stand a chance against his well-trained troops. It was bound to be a bloodbath.

'Never!' Birte shrieked back. 'We'd rather die!'

She raised the lucky latrine standard defiantly aloft. Her warriors were screaming insults at the enemy, waggling their bare bums.

'This is madness,' murmured Metellus. 'They're going to be massacred.' He admired their bravery. But his men would make short work of them and get the standard back.

But the troops weren't all as confident as their commander. There were some mutinous mutterings in the ranks. The loss of their lucky standard had shaken them badly.

A limping man was lagging behind: the soldier who'd been Finn's marching mate. The watchers in the grove heard him groan, 'I've got bad feet, somebody ate my blister stick and we lost our standard. This just isn't our lucky day.'

Briana whispered, 'I've got to go out there. Show Mum I'm free!'

'No!' hissed the Keeper, grabbing her arm. 'It's too dangerous.'

She'd have to run through the Roman army. They'd think she was one of the enemy and kill her immediately. There were plenty of women warriors among the painted people.

'Surrender!' yelled Metellus again. 'This is your last chance!' He didn't want to hurt them.

But Birte and her warriors were battle-crazed, working themselves up into a frenzy. They wouldn't listen to reason.

'Prepare to charge!' Metellus told his men.

'Let me go!' said Briana, struggling to break free of the Keeper's grip.

'Wait!' hissed the Keeper. 'There's another way.'

He talked in an urgent whisper to Nauseus.

The augur looked alarmed. 'You can do it,'
said the Keeper. 'I'll be right beside you.'
Nauseus looked reassured. Whenever he got
into a jam, his slave always got him out of it.

The Keeper shooed the hens outside. 'Want
any help?' asked Superloo. Maybe it could
send its voice booming out over the battlefield.
Command them to stop fighting. Surely they'd
listen to a god?

'Thanks, Divinity, but no thanks,' said the
Keeper. Water gods were about as reliable as
emperors. And this one had already caused
them enough trouble already.

'Just remember,' the Keeper told Nauseus.
'Make this your best performance ever.'

Together they walked, with the sacred
chickens fluttering around them, through the
soldiers.

Now they were in the empty space between
Birte and the cohort. Surprised, both sides
lowered their weapons. Silence fell.

The augur was trembling like a grass blade
in the wind.

'Courage, Master!' said the Keeper.

And suddenly Nauseus seemed to find
strength, as if he knew all eyes were on him,
that this was his chance to shine. His voice

wasn't vague or dithery when he spoke. For once, it was sure and certain. Standing tall in his flowing white toga, he addressed Metellus's men.

'This is a most inauspicious day to fight,' he told them. 'Behold my sacred chickens!'

He scattered some corn on the ground from his leather pouch.

But the chickens wouldn't even look at it. They just slumped on the ground in dismal, feathery heaps.

'See!' said Nauseus, in a voice that rang with authority. 'It couldn't be clearer. It would be folly to fight today. The gods do not favour you.'

'Just what I've been saying,' agreed the soldier with the bad feet. 'I've had nothing but rotten luck all day. I wish I'd stayed in bed.'

The Keeper was really impressed. His master didn't need his help. He was managing very well on his own. In fact, he was doing magnificently. His words were spreading through the ranks. 'The gods do not favour us.'

Metellus frowned. He appealed to his men, 'We must rescue our standard!' But even he was hesitating. You couldn't argue with sacred chickens.

From somewhere very close came an ear-splitting squawk: 'COCK-A-DOODLE-DOO!'

What's that? thought Finn.

Something burst into the grove in a flash of metallic green. Finn saw a loony eye, a bright red crest, scaly claws.

'The sacred cockerel,' said Briana. 'It's come back!'

Finn had thought Superloo was sulking because the Keeper refused its help. But suddenly it yakked, 'Catch it, Finn. If the sacred hens see it, they'll start feeding again.'

'What?' said Finn. 'What?' as the cockerel strutted about, pecking here and there, scratching the ground.

'Catch it,' commanded Superloo, more urgently. 'If you don't, people will die.'

Finn hurled himself heroically towards the bird. It crowed in fury, then hopped away in a glitter of green and purple. Beady eyes glared at him. 'Cock-a-doodle-doo!'

'Oh no, the hens will hear it. Drive it into me!' said Superloo.

'*Shoo! Shoo!*' said Finn, flapping his hands.

The cockerel poked its head round Superloo's door, and had a look. One scaly toe went in, then another.

'Gotcha!' said Superloo, sliding its door shut.

Briana and Finn turned anxiously back to see how Nauseus was doing. Behind them in the cubicle, the cockerel was going berserk. It hated to be confined, it liked to be wild and free. They heard frenzied crashings, bangings, strangled *cock-a-doodle-doos*. What was going on in there?

But Finn's eyes were fixed on the battlefield. Was there going to be a fight? Finn let out a slow sigh of relief. Nauseus had convinced the legionaries. Metellus's men were laying down their weapons.

But what about Birte? Would she back down? Her warriors were discussing it. One was leaving – 'I'm going to the pub.' Birte gave a shriek of rage. 'I still haven't got my daughter!' Seizing the lucky latrine standard in one hand and her sword in the other, she charged towards the cohort.

'That crazy woman,' sighed Metellus. But she was dangerous too; he had to protect his men. 'Archer!' he ordered. An auxiliary put an arrow in his bow.

'No!'

Before Finn could stop her, Briana had rushed out of the sacred grove and dashed through the cohort: 'Mother, it's me!' She and Birte met in the middle of the empty plain. As both sides looked on, Birte threw down her sword and gave her daughter a fierce bear hug. 'I thought I'd lost you!'

Mother and daughter clung to each other, both in tears. Even battle-hardened soldiers were touched: 'Awww.'

Metellus snapped another order to the archer, who put down his bow.

The Fort Commander thought about his own son, whom he'd last seen running from the cohort. Where was he now? *I'll have to organize a search party*, thought Metellus. Their meeting had been a disaster. *But what did you expect?* Metellus asked himself. *After thirteen years?* The boy and he were strangers to each other; they didn't even speak the same language. *When I find him again*, thought Metellus, watching Birte and Briana. *I'm going to hug him like that.*

But perhaps Flaccus would never be found. Perhaps he'd been killed by the painted people. Metellus couldn't bear to think about that.

'Please let him be alive,' he prayed. He'd give anything to see his son again, for a chance to make amends.

But a blaring trumpet brought his thoughts back to the battlefield. He'd thought it was all over – that there would be no fighting today. But over the hill tramped a formidable squad of soldiers. Tall, bristling with weapons, their armour polished to a silver dazzle, they were show-case troops, hand-picked by the Emperor, marching in perfect time.

'The Praetorian Guard,' gasped Metellus. The Emperor's bodyguard – what were they doing here?

But they'd seen Birte and her raggle-taggle band of warriors. They charged towards them in close formation. As one, their spears levelled, flashing in the sun.

Birte and her men hardly had time to react. They stood, open-mouthed, at this new menace appearing over the hill as if by magic. They were trapped anyway. The Wall was behind them, and the cohort was between them and the wilderness. There was nowhere left to run.

But still the Keeper yelled, 'Run, Briana!' There was going to be carnage. The Praetorian Guard was almost within spear-hurling distance when a voice roared from the fort ramparts. 'Stop! Your Emperor commands you!' A trumpet blast sounded the 'Cease Attack'. Were the guards going to stop? The painted people took up their weapons in a desperate attempt to defend themselves. But at the last moment the guards swerved and clashed to a halt. All eyes swivelled to the ramparts and the golden figure standing there. As one, they saluted, fists crashing on armour.

'Hadrian!' gasped Metellus. What was going on? As far as he knew, the Emperor wasn't due until tomorrow.

'Let the painted people live!' thundered the Emperor, in a voice used to being obeyed.

The Guard lowered their weapons.

'*Phew!*' gasped Finn from his hiding place. 'That was close.'

Everyone was staring at Hadrian as he strode from the fort with Sextus behind him, still carrying his net and trident.

Then the Keeper's sharp eyes noticed something. Some sentries from the fort were coming out too. But two of them weren't sentries. The Keeper saw a flash of daggers.

'Conspirators!' yelled the Keeper. It was the two men he'd seen outside the Temple of

Mithras. Their leader, Clavus, had been arrested. But they were determined to kill Hadrian, even if they died doing it.

Sextus reacted first. With that casual flick of the wrist he hurled his net. In a second, the two were tangled like flies in its meshes. The Praetorian Guard surrounded them.

'Well spotted, boy,' said Metellus, clapping the Keeper on the shoulder to congratulate him. He saw 'FUG' branded on the Keeper's forehead. 'Slave, I will see you get your freedom for this,' he said.

Briana spoke up. 'Sir, there is something you should know about the Keeper.'

The Keeper flashed her a warning glance but Briana didn't care – the truth had to be told.

'He is your true son,' she told Metellus.

Metellus stared at her, astonished. But there was no time to ask more questions. Hadrian was mounting his own horse, Velox, a noble beast, brought along by his Praetorian Guard. Metellus hurried over. 'Sir, aren't you staying?'

'I must leave immediately,' said Hadrian, turning his back. He'd had quite enough of this frontier fort at the edge of Empire. He wanted to get back to civilization and decent bathhouses. Places where they didn't use dormice to wipe their bums.

He gave orders to his Praetorian Guard. Two marched into the fort and came back with Clavus in chains.

Metellus said, 'Clavus, a prisoner?' He was totally confused.

Suddenly, a screech came from the wilderness. A figure staggered out.

'Scrofina!' said Metellus.

Scrofina had finally managed to escape from the bear. But her gown and her make-up were ruined. She was hopping mad.

'I'm sick to death of this dump!' she raved at Metellus. 'I'm sick of living among savages! I'm leaving you! I'm going back to Rome!'

She stomped into the fort. Metellus gazed after her. 'I don't understand,' he said. 'What's been going on here while I've been beyond the Wall?'

CHAPTER FIFTEEN

Hadrian rode off into the distance, with his Praetorian Guard marching after him. They took the three conspirators with them. And Scrofina had begged to go too. She was bringing up the rear in her litter, carried by sweating servants, with four ox carts loaded with all her gowns and jewellery.

'Take me with you, Emperor!' she'd screeched. And Hadrian had had to agree, just to give his ears a rest.

The last thing he did before he left was promise Sextus a small farm, as a reward for netting the two conspirators. He seemed to forget that the Keeper had spotted them first.

The noise of blaring trumpets, the glitter of golden armour faded – the Emperor had gone. The cohort marched back into the fort. The painted warriors melted into the wilderness. Now only a small group was left: the Keeper and Briana, Sextus, Metellus and Birte. And Nauseus, with his sad sacred chickens.

Finn peeped out from the grove. The lucky latrine standard was lying in the heather where Birte had dropped it, so that she could give her daughter a big hug. Had it been forgotten? A little voice urged, inside Finn's head, 'You could nip out and nick it! Go on, do it now! Think how chuffed Superloo would be!'

But the standard hadn't been forgotten. Suddenly Birte picked it up. She'd got her daughter back, there was no point in any more fighting. And besides, although it was a great prize, she didn't want a loo seat hanging above her hut door, along with her lucky heads. That would be in very bad taste.

With a solemn gesture she handed the standard back to Metellus. He accepted it graciously. Then saluted. Peace had broken out. Now everyone was talking at once, explanations flying backwards and forwards. Metellus looked at the Keeper's charm, at the faded picture of his first wife. He must have believed Briana because Finn saw him give the Keeper a bear hug that almost lifted him off his feet.

He saw a big smile replace the uncertainty on the Keeper's face.

Awww! thought Finn. *I love happy endings.*

And then Metellus did something else. To honour the Keeper's courage, he took a wreath from the cohort's lucky latrine standard and placed it on his son's forehead. It covered 'FUG' completely. Now no one would know it was there.

'Your baby name was Flaccus,' Metellus told his son. '*He with the sticky-out ears.* But that's no name for a soldier. The name you have now is better. *Custos*, the Keeper, the Protector.'

Finn, watching from the trees, was glad that his chance to pinch the standard was gone. In his heart, he knew Superloo shouldn't have it. That it should stay here, at the fort. Perhaps, one day, the Keeper would march out before it, proudly leading the cohort, just like his father did now.

And, all at once, Finn felt terribly lonely and left out. For a few hours he'd been part of Roman Britain. But now all he wanted to do was go home, to his own family, where he belonged, where he understood what people were saying. He wanted to do ordinary things: play computer games in his own bedroom;

take a triple cheese, deep-crust pizza from the freezer and smell it cooking in the oven.

He put up his duffel-coat hood and shrank back into the grove.

'Let me in,' he said to Superloo.

Superloo's door slid open. Finn went in warily.

'Where's the cockerel?' he asked, surprised.

There were feathers on the floor, glittering purple and green, peck marks on the mirror where it had fought its own reflection, shredded toilet paper scattered about like confetti. But of the bird itself there was no sign.

'Look what a mess it's made!' complained Superloo. 'I tried to calm it down. I played it "Drip, drip, drop little April showers". But that seemed to make it even madder.'

'So what did you do with it?' asked Finn. He had a sudden frightful thought. 'You didn't flush it down the toilet bowl, did you?'

'*Cha!*' said Superloo. 'What do you take me for? Besides, it would have blocked my U-bend. No, I shut it up in my storage compartment.'

'How did you do that?' asked Finn, impressed.

'My floor moves, remember,' said Superloo smugly. 'Look, I'll give you a quick demo.'

'*Aaargh*,' cried Finn, his arms whirling like windmills as the floor slid away under his feet. Wobbling wildly, he was carried, as if on a conveyor belt, from one side of the cubicle to the other. As he neared the cupboard, Superloo opened the door.

'*Aaargh!*' yelled Finn again, as the sacred rooster exploded out like a green-and-purple firework. It shot over his head, almost parting his hair, and disappeared into the trees.

'It's found the hens,' said Finn, after a few seconds. He could hear their glad clucking as they crowded round the cockerel.

'They're welcome to it,' said Superloo. 'That bird's a lunatic.'

Nauseus looked down happily. All his sacred chickens were pecking around his feet. They were certainly packing that seed away! Even he couldn't mistake what that meant. It was amazing how quickly fortune changed.

'Now this is a very *auspicious* day,' said the augur.

He felt pleased with himself and full of a new self-confidence. He'd been right two times in one day! He was finally getting good at this augury business. He even thought he could manage without the Keeper. So long as he stuck to predictions with sacred chickens and didn't do any gut-gazing.

'Let's go back into the fort and eat that banquet,' said Metellus. It seemed a shame for it to go to waste.

Finn watched the little group of five people, with the happy sacred chickens fluttering behind, walk towards the North Gate of the fort and out of his life. Sextus was chatting up Birte, checking his hair in his little bronze mirror. He wasn't a gladiator any more – but old habits die hard.

'How are they doing?' asked Superloo. 'Do they need my help?'

Finn stared at Superloo in surprise. He'd thought the great toilet genius didn't care about humans.

'They're doing all right,' answered Finn gruffly. 'They don't need us.'

'Oh, right,' said Superloo, sounding rather hurt.

And Finn couldn't help it – he felt upset too, as they turned their backs. But if even the water god had slipped their mind, why should they remember him, a mere servant?

Then, at the last moment, the Keeper and Briana turned round.

'*Vale!*' shouted the Keeper. 'Farewell, Finn!' He gave a soldier's salute and Briana gave a wave before they vanished into the fort.

'Time to go home,' said Finn. 'And don't start arguing about the lucky latrine standard,' he warned Superloo.

He'd steeled himself for tears, threats, sulks. But all Superloo said was, 'You win some, you lose some.'

'You don't mind?' asked Finn, amazed. 'You don't mind leaving your toilet relative behind?'

'I do *mind*,' admitted Superloo. 'I mind awfully. But it wouldn't be right to take it. It belongs with the cohort.'

'That's just what I thought,' said Finn, surprised that the toilet shared his feelings. Sometimes, he could swear it was almost human.

'Blast off again then?' said Superloo.

My dormice! thought Finn. Should he leave them behind in Roman Britain, where they belonged? No way, he decided. They might get stuffed and roasted for some posh person's banquet. They'd have to come back with him to the twenty-first century. They were his responsibility now.

'I'm ready,' said Finn grimly.

There was the usual hollow feeling in the

pit of his stomach. But it wasn't just Superloo rotating. Finn felt a bit flat and empty after all the excitement. The others, back at the fort, were celebrating. Sextus had his farm and his freedom, the Keeper had found his father, and Briana and Birte were best friends again. Finn wanted something to celebrate too. Instead, he was stuck in a public convenience, clinging to a toilet bowl.

As if it could read his mind, Superloo suddenly stopped. It slid its cubicle door open, just a fraction.

'Look outside,' it said.

'What?' said Finn. 'Are we home already?'

He crawled to the door and peered through the gap. There was nothing but blue. Then a wisp of cloud drifted in; he was eye-to-eye with a seagull! He scuttled back to the toilet bowl. 'We're in mid-air!'

'I know,' said Superloo. 'But before we left Roman Britain behind forever, I wanted you to see something. Look down.'

Finn squirmed back to the door, commando style. He looked dizzily down. 'It's the Wall.' The Wall in winter sunshine, snaking away over the crags. All the white-wash had worn off, it was grey again, dusted with a light sprinkling of snow, like icing sugar.

'Are there people down there?' asked Superloo.

'Yeah, there's a sentry patrolling along the Wall. He's wearing a *Birrus Britannicus* to keep him warm.'

'Notice anything special about it?'

'No,' said Finn, puzzled. Then, 'Wait a minute!' he yelled, almost falling out of the door in excitement. 'He's got toggles! And there's a woman with a water pot. And some kids collecting firewood. They've got toggles too! *Everyone's* got toggles!'

'And who do you think started the craze?'

'I don't know,' said Finn.

'Do I have to spell it out?' asked Superloo impatiently. 'Remember how those ladies were dead interested in your toggles? Well, those same ladies rushed straight home. They made their own toggles. Used them for fastenings instead of brooches. Soon everyone wanted them. The whole of Britannica became toggle-mad!'

'Wow!' said Finn, finally catching on. 'Wow! Was that really all down to *me*?'

'Of course,' said Superloo. 'History books tell us the Romans introduced toggles to Roman Britain. But they know *nothing*. It was you – Finn Gallaghan of 22, Cedar Gardens.'

The door closed again. Finn went back to hang on to the toilet bowl. But now he too had something to celebrate.

I'm the kid who brought toggles to Roman Britain, he thought, amazed. He was famous. Even if nobody knew but him and Superloo.

'Thanks for showing me,' he told Superloo. 'I needed cheering up.'

'I know,' replied Superloo simply. It began to twirl again. 'And now we're *really* going home.'

They landed, with the usual bone-shaking thump. Finn slid off the wall, where he'd been stuck like a fridge magnet.

'We've arrived,' said Superloo. Its voice sounded slow and woozy. After the trip back its power was always low. It shouldn't have stopped to show Finn those toggles. That had reduced its power to dangerous levels.

Finn was checking his dormice – incredibly, those fat little fur balls were still snoozing – when there was an urgent hammering on Superloo's door. A muffled voice was shouting something.

Superloo hardly had the energy to slide its door open. Mr Lew Brush burst in.

'Quick,' he told Superloo, 'you can't stay here. The place is swarming with Special Forces!'

CHAPTER SIXTEEN

This time Superloo couldn't protest. It didn't have the power to be bossy or argue. It couldn't even retract into its underground den. Its systems were barely operable. It would have to depend on humans to protect it.

'Come on, Finn,' said Mr Lew Brush. 'We haven't much time. They're coming this way.'

Finn stepped out of the cubicle. 'Where'd you get this?' he said, staring upwards. It was a bright yellow monster all-terrain truck with a crane on the back.

'From Hi-Tech Toilets,' said Mr Lew Brush. 'They use them for moving their public conveniences.'

His knees creaked as he climbed into the cab. He'd driven the crane here at breakneck speed, then off-roaded it through the disused industrial site.

'How do you know the Special Forces are coming this way?' asked Finn. The weeds and rubble heaps seemed quiet and peaceful in the late afternoon sunshine.

'Because the long, lonely howl of the Bog Hound has stopped,' said Mr Brush.

That meant they'd finally found Blaster, not at the nearest public convenience, like Mr Brush had promised, but slumped in a wailing heap somewhere. And now, Mr Brush guessed, they were leading him back this way. That smart young lieutenant would start asking some awkward questions. They'd already been suspicious about what was under that corrugated-iron sheet.

'Pardon?' said Finn screwing up his face in bewilderment. 'Howl? Bog Hound?' He hadn't understood any of that.

'Never mind,' said Mr Brush. 'I'll explain later.' He gripped a lever in the cab. 'Watch out!' The crane swung round. Its great metal jaws locked round Superloo, hoisting it upwards.

As it dangled in mid-air, did Superloo sense the indignity of its position? A muffled protest came from inside. 'This is no way to treat a water god!'

There was more grinding of machinery as the crane dumped Superloo on the back of the truck.

'Quick,' said Mr Lew Brush as he climbed down. 'Help me cover it up.' From the cab he'd seen the tall grasses rippling, as if men were crawling through them. 'They're almost here.'

He and Finn hauled a tarpaulin over Superloo and re-covered its underground den with the iron sheet. They were standing beside the truck, looking innocent, when the first soldier broke cover.

As Mr Lew Brush predicted, they had Blaster with them. The old hound whimpered with joy when he saw his master, shambled up and slobbered over his hand.

They've got guns, thought Finn, dismayed. And all sorts of hi-tech searching gear. It looked like they meant business. Someone wanted Superloo's microchip brain very badly.

'I think you should stop playing games with us, sir,' the young lieutenant suggested to Mr Brush. His voice sounded as polite as ever. But his eyes were hard and suspicious.

'Playing games?' quavered Mr Brush, putting on his daft old codger act.

'Yeah,' interrupted another soldier. 'This

Bog Hound is no good. He led us precisely nowhere.'

'And what's this?'

Finn's heartbeat went into overdrive as another soldier strode over and lifted up the tarpaulin a little. 'Hey, Lieutenant, looks like there's a public convenience under here.'

The young lieutenant stared at Mr Lew Brush, 'Sir, would you like to tell us what's going on?'

Mr Brush looked dopey. But inside his head his brain was working at top speed. His eyes glittered briefly – this was going to be a challenge. He said, 'It's my training loo.'

'What?' said the lieutenant.

'The loo I use to train my young Bog Hounds. Blaster here is getting old and tired. Like you saw yourself, sometimes he's just not up to the job. So I'm training some new Bog Hounds to take over. I drive this loo to places. Then set them loose to track it.'

'That's a good idea,' said the friendly soldier who wanted to start up his own Bog Hound business.

But the young lieutenant didn't seem convinced. 'I think we'll take a look at your training loo,' he said.

Oh no, thought Finn. His stomach scrunched into knots – he felt sick. Nothing could save Superloo now.

But Mr Brush was speaking again. 'Help yourself,' he shrugged, as if he'd got nothing to hide. 'But I presume the public convenience you're looking for is state of the art, the very latest design?'

'Yes, it is,' agreed the lieutenant.

The MD at Hi-Tech Toilets had briefed him. 'My company's loos are something special,' he'd said. 'You can't mistake them.' He'd shown the lieutenant pictures – the Hi-Tech Toilet loos were like sleek, silver-space-age pods.

'See for yourself,' said Mr Brush, lifting up the tarpaulin further to show Superloo's sides, scarred and dented from Birte's sword attack. 'This one is just an old reject I bought second-hand.'

'An old reject!' came a feeble squawk from inside Superloo. But from the first syllable Finn was coughing and choking to smother the sound. He just knew that toilet couldn't keep quiet.

'You all right, son?' said a soldier, thumping Finn on the back as he spluttered, red-faced.

'*Hummmm*,' mused the young lieutenant, tapping his shiny boots. That loo certainly looked nothing at all like the pictures. He considered some more and said finally, 'You're free to go, sir.'

As he climbed in the cab with Finn and Blaster, Mr Brush gave a long, ragged sigh of relief. He took off like a boy racer in the monster truck, in case that young lieutenant changed his mind.

CHAPTER SEVENTEEN

The next day, Finn was sitting in the Toilet Museum. Superloo was full of beans, back to its usual bouncy, know-it-all self, with its computer brain buzzing. Mr Lew Brush had connected it to the mains overnight to re-charge it.

'You're safe here,' Mr Brush told the toilet genius. 'This is the last place they'll think you'll hide.'

Mr Brush seemed to have forgotten all about the bum-wiping sponge. He had two much more exciting new exhibits. He was polishing them now: King Tut's toilet and Hadrian's golden latrine.

'It's a privilege,' Mr Brush told Superloo, 'to have your toilet ancestors in my museum.'

He didn't even mind that Finn's dormice had chewed through a pocket of his duffel coat. It was so moth-eaten anyway, what difference would one more hole make?

But, for Finn, those dormice were a big worry. He knew he should release them back into the wild. But how could he? They were so unfit, they couldn't escape from predators. They'd be scoffed straight away by a weasel or sparrowhawk.

He was watching them now. He'd set up a dormouse gym in Blaster's old dog basket: ladders, a hamster wheel, a tiny trampoline. But they weren't working out at all; they just lay in a furry heap, snoring their heads off.

Finn sighed. They weren't going to lose weight through exercise. He'd just have to be strict with their diet.

'No more walnuts,' said Finn sternly to the roly-poly rodents. It'd just be low-calorie snacks like lettuce leaves from now on.

At least Finn's other worry was sorted out. Last night he'd asked, 'Mum, do I have sticky-out ears? Be honest! I want to know the truth!'

'Of course you don't, darling,' Mum had said, without bothering to look. 'Your ears are perfectly fine.'

So that was a load off his mind.

Mr Lew Brush and Superloo had big plans for the Toilet Museum. They were talking about them now.

'I want this to be an *International* Toilet Museum,' said Mr Brush. 'And welcome people from all over the world.'

'Of course,' yakked Superloo, 'that means you'll have to make it child-friendly.'

'How do I do that?' asked Mr Brush, who hadn't a clue what children liked.

For once, Superloo had no opinion. It didn't know much about children either. In fact, it found the whole human species a big mystery.

'Wait a minute,' it said, 'why don't we ask Finn? He's a child, isn't he?'

Finn was flattered. The toilet genius was an expert on everything – yet it needed his advice!

'Well,' said Finn, thinking hard, 'you've got to make it interactive. So kids can feel *part* of it, you know, play games and stuff.'

'Games?' said Superloo. It searched its data banks for games that were toilet-related. 'I've found one!' it crowed triumphantly. 'What about Pooh Sticks?'

'Pardon?' said Finn.

'Pooh Sticks. Surely that involves toilets?'

'No,' said Finn, 'it's got nothing to do with

toilets. Pooh is the name of a *teddy bear* and the game is about racing your sticks down a river.'

What kind of children's game had Superloo imagined? Finn shuddered. *Don't go there*, he warned himself. He didn't even want to *think* about it.

While Finn explained about Pooh Sticks, the Managing Director of Hi-Tech Toilets was staring out of his office window. Behind his modern factory he could see the crumbling roof of the Toilet Museum. It reminded him of something he'd been meaning to do for some time.

I must close that place down, he thought. *Get rid of that bolshy caretaker and his crusty old dog. And that disgusting ancient toilet collection.*

It was hardly a good advert for his sleek, modern, hygienic loos. He wrote a note to himself on his memo pad, so he wouldn't forget.

Superloo was surrounded by dangers. It was being hunted down by crack troops who wanted to terminate it. The very building it had taken refuge in might soon be demolished. But you wouldn't have known it. The toilet genius was in a bright and bubbly mood. It was as excited as a child at Christmas.

'Oh no,' groaned Finn. He knew the signs. Superloo had been using its massive brain to do some historical research. It had found another toilet ancestor who needed rescuing.

'You're not planning another mission, are you?' asked Finn suspiciously. He was still recovering from the last one. 'Being taken out on patrol with the Roman army was no picnic, you know,' he reminded Superloo.

'But this trip will be easy-peasy,' said the toilet in honeyed tones. 'It'll be a walk in the park, a breeze! Oh, *doooo* come,' coaxed Superloo.

'*No, no, no, no,*' said Finn, shaking his head so hard it almost fell off. 'You can cry, you can shout, you can sulk, I don't care. Count me out. No way. Next time I absolutely, *definitely,* won't be coming!'

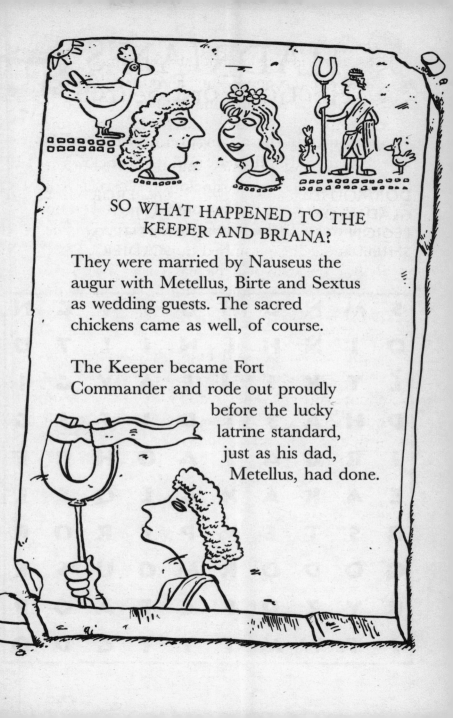

SO WHAT HAPPENED TO THE KEEPER AND BRIANA?

They were married by Nauseus the augur with Metellus, Birte and Sextus as wedding guests. The sacred chickens came as well, of course.

The Keeper became Fort Commander and rode out proudly before the lucky latrine standard, just as his dad, Metellus, had done.

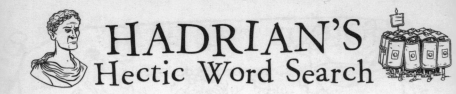

HADRIAN'S
Hectic Word Search

Finn met all these things on his time travels.
Can you find them in the grid below?

DORMOUSE   EMPEROR
GLADIATOR   LATIN
LEGION   MITHRAS
SHIELD   SOLDIER

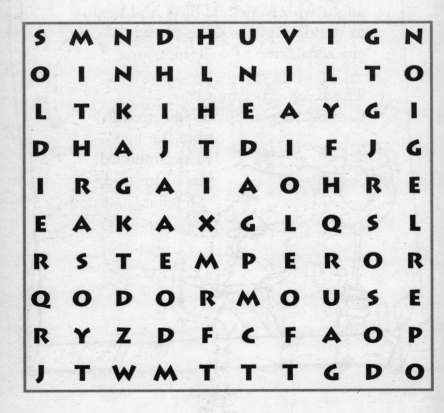

S	M	N	D	H	U	V	I	G	N
O	I	N	H	L	N	I	L	T	O
L	T	K	I	H	E	A	Y	G	I
D	H	A	J	T	D	I	F	J	G
I	R	G	A	I	A	O	H	R	E
E	A	K	A	X	G	L	Q	S	L
R	S	T	E	M	P	E	R	O	R
Q	O	D	O	R	M	O	U	S	E
R	Y	Z	D	F	C	F	A	O	P
J	T	W	M	T	T	T	G	D	O

ROUND THE BEND

Someone's dropped a dormouse
down the loo! But which one?

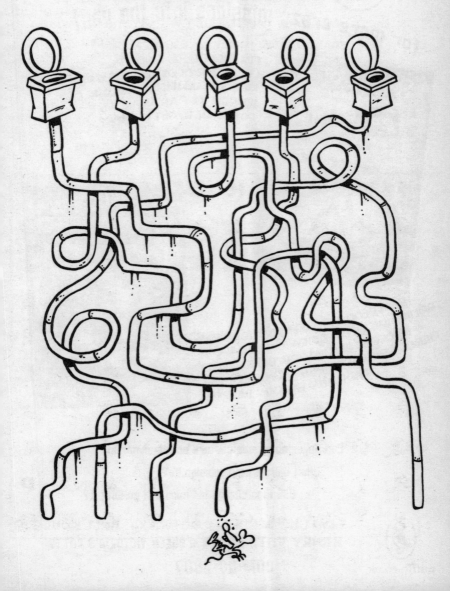

Join **SUPERLOO**

for more crazy missions into the past...

FINN NEEDS TO FIND THE LEGENDARY GOLDEN TOILET OF KING TUTANKHAMUN – CAN HE PASS HIMSELF OFF AS AN ANCIENT EGYPTIAN TO GET IT BACK?

SUPERLOO HAS TAKEN FINN TO ROMAN BRITAIN WHERE CONSPIRACIES ARE AFOOT INVOLVING GLADIATORS, BEARS, VERY FIERCE BRITISH TRIBES AND, OF COURSE ... HADRIAN'S FAMOUS LATRINE.

Can Superloo escape capture and termination?

What will its next mission be?

Will Finn change his mind and go with it?

FIND OUT IN SUPERLOO'S NEXT TOILET QUESTS:
HENRY VIII'S PRIVY & **QUEEN VICTORIA'S POTTY**
COMING 2007

puffin.co.uk